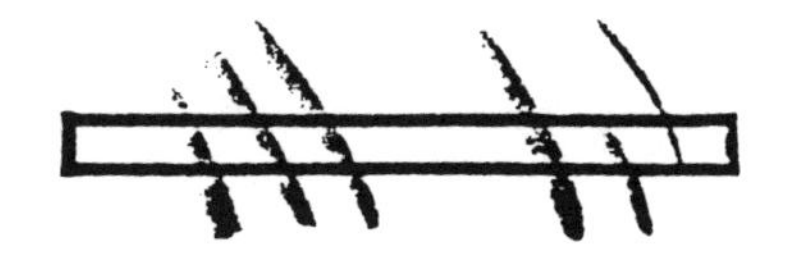

SEASONAL RAIN

AND OTHER STORIES

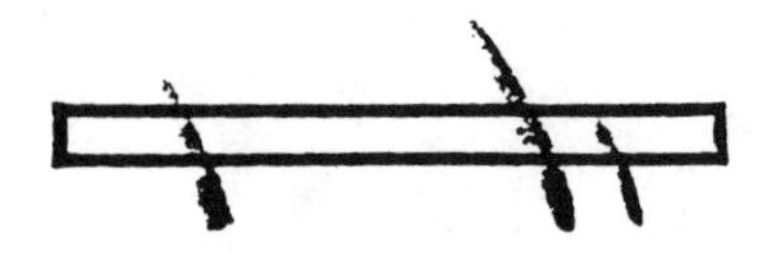

Other books by Robert Flynn:

North To Yesterday (1967)
In the House of the Lord (1969)
The Sounds of Rescue,
The Signs of Hope (1970)

SEASONAL RAIN

AND OTHER STORIES BY ROBERT FLYNN

CORONA / DAVID BOWEN
SAN ANTONIO 1986

For information address
Corona Publishing Company,
1037 South Alamo, San Antonio, Texas 78210

Library of Congress Catalog Card Number 86-70716
ISBN 0-931722-57-8 (cloth)
ISBN 0-931722-60-8 (paper)

Book design by Lyn Belisle

Printed and bound in the United States of America

To my sister Bettye

Six of these stories have appeared in other publications: "The Saviour of the Bees"—PEN/NEA Syndicated Fiction Project, "The Boy from Chillicothe"—*Yale Review*, "Waiting for the Postman"—*Pawn Review*, "The Killer"—*Vietnam Flashbacks* (anthology published by Pig Iron Press and the National Endowment for the Arts), "Christmas in a Very Small Place"—PEN/NEA Syndicated Fiction Project, "Seasonal Rain" —*Greensboro Review*.

CONTENTS

INTRODUCTION

Wisdom consists in knowing the season, knowing when to fight and when to make accommodations, when to take hold and when to let go. That is the dichotomy of this book, and the tension on which the stories hang together.

Rain is one of the blessings of earth, the salvation of the farmer, but hell to the infantryman. But even to the farmer, rain at the wrong time, out of season, is destructive. We say both "welcome as summer rain," and "into every life a little rain must fall." There is also a dichotomy in the harvest. The harvest is a time of fulfillment, of rejoicing, but death is the Grim Reaper, and war is the random harvest.

These stories are about people who experience rain in their lives, "seasonal rain" because rain is to be expected, and also because it lasts only for a season. Even the Turrills, who have suffered through a great deal of rain, can find beauty in their lives. And Chris discovers that rain for him, and for the other soldiers, is for a season. The time to kill passes and the time to heal begins.

All of the characters endure rain, all of them find an accommodation with the cycles, the seasons. There is of course another word play on "seasonal." The characters by enduring become "seasoned" veterans. They gain flavor, character. And because of that they will not only endure. The rain will come again but they will prevail.

SEASONAL RAIN

AND OTHER STORIES

THE MIDNIGHT CLEAR

She was almost thirty-seven and out of time. Like others she had wanted children, a husband, a home. Like others she had a hope chest, embroidered dreams, crocheted illusions. Like others she had expectations. She wanted a man who was clean, polite but not fawning, educated but not vain about it, gentle but not weak, not given to snuff or overly given to alcohol, sloth, and smiling at women. In two months she would be up to hopeless, and her expectations down to clean.

At her feet, under the still fresh mound of dirt and already dusty bits of ribbon was her father. A hard man—some said selfish. A religious man—some said self-righteous. Her mother had died when she was twelve and she had taken on her mother's work of taking care of him. He frequently quoted the Bible regarding a virtuous woman and a daughter's duty towards her father.

Standing over his grave, she felt an emptiness in the place where duty had been, a sadness where love had been, a pain where anger had been, and a blank where hope had been. She shook the dust off the ribbons and retied them to the wooden cross where she had placed them for a bit of color. She had taken the ribbons off the Christmas tree. Her father wasn't much for frivolity but being a Christian he let her decorate a Christmas tree. It was still five days until Christmas but she wouldn't be needing the ribbons. Or the tree. She had been loved and ill-used. Now she was alone.

He was almost forty-five and almost out of luck. Like others he had wanted a piece of land, a strong, healthy wife, and a passel of hearty, handy kids to help with the work. Like others he had prospects—a Peter Shutter wagon, a good team of mules, and the money. Like others he had expectations—a woman old enough not to be flighty, not too old to work and have kids; girl enough to be tender-hearted but woman enough not to be weepy; not so pretty as to be spoiled or so ugly as to be mean; not too fast out of bed to be a comfort, or too slow to have coffee ready by first light when it was time to go to work; not so big as to be clumsy or so small as to be worthless with mules or the bearer of children too small to handle posthole diggers.

At his feet, under the still-fresh mound of dirt and the flowers and feathers he had taken off her hats, was his wife. She had been pretty—some said frail. She had been cheerful—some said giddy. She had told him she loved him and sung him songs while the biscuits burned, the garden went un-dug, and he had to hire a hand to help him castrate his calves, survey his fence lines, and scald his hogs.

Standing over her grave he felt emptiness where the impatience had been, grief where the love had been, emptiness where the disappointment had been, dead where the dreams had been. He had been loved but not helped, and now he was alone.

He noticed her because she was crying softly and trying to retie the red and green ribbons so they did not tangle in the wind. She was healthy. She noticed him because he had tears in his eyes and was trying to keep the little bouquet of feathers and flowers from blowing off the grave. He was clean. She stood and the ribbons tangled until they looked like something that had been discarded. He stood up and the feathers blew away and the flowers rolled up at his feet.

"I got a hammer and some nails in the wagon if that will help you," he said, holding his hat in his hand. He had feelings.

"I'm obliged. I got a pin if you can use it," she said. She knew how to use a hammer.

She watched him as he gathered the feathers and flowers and deftly pinned them together. He had gentle hands.

He watched as she drove nails into the wooden cross and rearranged the ribbons. She was strong and definite.

"I got a little something to eat if you'd like a bite," she said. She had brought a basket from town. A generous woman.

"I got some water in the wagon," he said. "And two cups." A thoughtful man.

While they ate, they talked. He had sold everything he had and was on his way to Wanderer Springs. He had hung on longer than he had intended, waiting for his wife to get strong enough to move. "Time to make a new start," he said.

She had spent her life taking care of her father. "I ain't never been alone," she said.

"What was your wife like?" she asked.

"She was a good woman, but made for gentler use than I could afford. What was your pa like?"

"He meant to get the most out of what was his whether it was a horse or a mule, but he was fair. He expected the same from everybody."

"I got money for a good farm," he said. "I'm a hard worker and a good farmer. I aim to get me a new wife and a passel of kids."

"I'm partial to kids," she said. "I ain't never been sick to speak of. I got all my teeth. I kept my own hens, weeded my own garden, milked my own cow, and helped Pa with the hitching, fencing, and loading."

"Would you be agreeable to marrying me?" he asked. His hat was in his hand again.

"I ain't never been married," she said.

"I ain't no fool boy to be rushing you," he said.

"How soon do you intend to start with the mothering and fathering?"

"I'd be willing to wait until we got to Wanderer Springs. It ain't but six days. If we got married today we could be there by Christmas." He turned and looked at the wagon, hitched and loaded and ready to go.

"Yes," she said. "I know where the preacher is. But it ain't but five days until Christmas."

They went by her house and got her hope chest, stood

before the preacher, and started for Wanderer Springs with her holding a bouquet made of the funeral flowers and the Christmas ribbons, and her cow tied to the back of the wagon.

The first day they talked about the house. "Lean-to is easiest," he said.

"Not for kids," she said.

They settled on a lean-to until the well was dug, three rooms before the second child, a storm cellar when the barn was finished, a well house when the fences were done, and a porch before the second barn.

He stopped the wagon at dusk. He built a fire while she milked the cow. While she cooked, he unharnessed the team and staked them out with the cow. They ate quickly in silence using syrup bucket lids for plates. The hope chest would not be unpacked until there was a lean-to. She asked if he had enough to eat and he said yes.

While she scoured the dishes with clean sand, he brought up more firewood and got the blankets out of the wagon. He spread her blankets before the fire and took his to the other side of the wagon. She lay down, fully clothed, and rolled her back to the fire. She saw him watching her from his bed on the other side of the wagon.

"I'd like to be hitched by first light," he said.

"Will the smell of coffee wake you?" she asked.

The second day they talked about the children. The first boy would be named for her dead father. The first girl would be named for his dead wife. If there wasn't a school by the time the first child was ten they would mail-order books and instead of picking berries she would teach them to read, write, and add, cook, can, and milk. Instead of fishing, he would teach them time, calendar, planting and harvesting season, sawing, fencing, and water witching. That night they slept on opposite sides of the wagon but he asked if she had enough wood. She said yes.

The third day they talked church. "I'm Baptist," she said. "I don't tolerate dipping, drinking, or dancing."

"I'm agreeable to church but I ain't no particular brand," he said. "I don't chew or drink, I don't cuss unless I have to, and I ain't never had no time for dancing."

She wanted grace before meals and reading the Bible to the children before bed. She could say grace before meals, he would read the Bible to the children, but he would not sing, pray, or testify in front of a bunch of Baptists. She would tithe eggs and butter to the preacher, he would pledge corn or cash to the church. That night they slept on separate sides of the wagon but he asked if she was warm enough. She said yes.

"We'll be on our own land by Christmas," he said. "Three more days."

"Christmas is day after tomorrow," she said.

"Today is Wednesday," he said.

"Today is Thursday."

The next day they were discussing whether to cure ham or smoke it. He said he didn't like ham as dry as that coyote they saw yesterday.

"What coyote?"

"That dead coyote that we passed by that little draw."

"Surely you mean wolf," she said. "It wasn't fullgrowned but it was a wolf."

"The one that was right there by the off-mule?" he said. "That was a coyote. I've knowed coyotes all my life."

"I was closer," she said.

For a while they sat in silence, listening to the grinding of the wheels, the jingle of the trace chains, the steady plodding of the mules. Then without a word he turned the wagon and they started on the back track. That night they slept on separate sides of the wagon.

The next day he clucked up the mules and they started up the back track. They didn't talk, lost in their own thoughts. He didn't want to be married to no stubborn, grudge-bearing woman. She didn't want to be married to no hard-headed man without the common sense to admit when he was wrong.

It was late afternoon when they reached the carcass and scavengers had scattered the bones. Both of them stood looking at it for a while and then he got the shotgun out of the wagon and started off down the draw. She got the axe and went in the opposite direction.

"I couldn't get no goose," he said. "All I got was a rabbit. I reckon that dog was chasing a rabbit when it died right over there."

"I'm partial to rabbit," she said. She propped up a salt cedar with rocks. She had decorated the tree with the ribbons and flowers from her bridal bouquet. "I got the tree ready 'cause we won't know when midnight comes," she said.

They ate the rabbit, and when they were finished, he said, "I didn't have no time for a proper gift. I'd like our first girl to be named for you."

"I think that's the nicest present I ever got," she said. "We'll name the second one for your first wife."

She scoured the pots with sand and he built up the fire and got the bedding out of the wagon.

"I didn't have no time for a proper gift for you," she said, "but I'd be proud if you spread your bed by the fire."

He looked at her for a moment, then spread the beds side by side before the fire. "Don't worry none about coffee in the morning," he said.

The Great Plain

Grover and Edna married, when Grover Turrill was sixteen, at the request of both families. Crowded out by younger children they set out for a life on their own. Grover's father gave them a milk cow and Edna's father gave them a steer. It was the best their families could do. Grover yoked the cow and steer together and they started to California in a wagon. It was his promise to Edna.

They crossed Red River and stopped near Preston where Edna had a baby boy with no one to help her but Grover. They named him Grover, too. They started moving again as soon as Edna was able to travel, Edna and the baby in the wagon, and Grover walking beside the wagon, prodding the ox and milk cow, and picking up firewood. After Preston there was little wood and Grover picked up whatever sticks he saw for the evening fire.

One day, tired of sitting, Edna placed the sleeping baby in the back of the wagon and got out to walk beside the cow. Grover found a tree stump and, not knowing the baby was in the back of the wagon, he threw in the stump, killing his child. Some cowboys found them, two teenagers traveling across the prairie with a dead baby wrapped in a quilt and carried in Edna's lap.

The cowboys dug a grave and buried the child, still wrapped in the quilt Edna's mother had given them. After the cowboys had gone, Grover and Edna made a cross of two pieces of firewood. For a long time they sat by the grave, trying to decide whether to abandon the grave of their first-born. Despite their youth their faces were lined and drawn. Already they were beginning to share that common look that was supposed to come only with years of togetherness.

"California is purty," Grover said, renewing his plight. Grover had been stunted and hardened by a life of misfortune, but Edna's steel had been warmed by motherhood. "It'll be easier to forget."

"We still got four hours of daylight," Edna said, getting to her feet. Her eyes acknowledged that life was hard, but her jaw was set for the long haul as she turned her face forever from the grave of her son.

Grover and Edna were still on their way to California when the milk cow died near Wanderer Springs. They lived in the wagon while Grover broke the land, with the steer and Edna pulling the plow, and planted a crop. The corn was to buy oxen to take them to California. Grover had a good harvest and Edna had a baby girl named Polly. The wagon was no place for a mother and baby. Grover built a lean-to for the winter.

In the spring Grover and the steer pulled, and Edna plowed, leaving the baby at the end of the row. By fall there was enough corn for an ox, but Edna had another son, this one called Billo. Grover traded the corn for a milk cow. He enclosed the lean-to and put in a door.

The land Grover had chosen was not good enough to make him forget his dreams, not rich enough to provide the means to accomplish it. There was always enough but the more than enough was soon required by boils, fevers, broken bones. Drought alternated with flood. Hail alternated with grasshoppers. There was high wind, early frost, unseasonal rain. Grover and Edna still talked of California but they built a regular house for the children. Grover traded the harvest for mules to pull the plow.

Others came to settle the land, break the soil, to share the joys and trials. While the children played, the adults talked about the friends and family they had left never to see again, and the freedom they hoped to find in the hard land. They sat or squatted near the earth, looking out across the prairie that was as silent and empty as a dream. They waited for the sun to fade and the wind to rise. "Best time of the day," they said.

Edna told of the gentle life Grover had promised her in California. "It's purty," Grover said. But the son they had left behind was buried in their own hearts.

Billo was small and tough like his father, and like his father, he was always in a hurry. When he was eight, Billo went coon hunting one night with some older boys. They ran a coon up a dead tree on the creek, and Billo climbed the tree to shake the coon down. A pile of brush had been washed up under the tree and the older boys set it afire so that Billo could see. The dead tree caught fire and Billo was burned so that he couldn't lie down and Edna and Grover took turns holding him the four days it took him to die.

The neighbors came to tend the fields and livestock, to look after Polly, and to feed Edna and Grover, who sat like double images, their faces set to bear all, do all, to spare Billo pain. They scarcely moved except to shift Billo from one lap to another.

When Billo died, the neighbors dug his grave, and Grover took him from Edna and laid him in it. The neighbors buried him, and sat for a while with Edna, and Grover, and Polly. They stared at the unforgiving earth and talked of the land where Billo had gone, a land without memory, without tears.

When the neighbors had gone, Edna and Grover held Polly close and told her of California and the sweetness of life there. "It's purty," Grover said.

"When?" Polly asked.

"As soon as I sell the land we'll have enough to go," Grover said.

When Polly was thirteen, she complained of a stomachache. Polly was not fat but, like Edna, she was slope-shouldered, solid, and a good eater. Polly was no whiner, but she tossed all night on her bed and was unable to eat breakfast. Grover hitched the team to the wagon, made a pallet in the back, and with Edna to comfort Polly they started for the doctor at Wanderer Springs, several miles away. The wagon had no springs, the road was just a set of ruts across the prairie. Polly whimpered the whole way although Grover drove as slowly as he dared.

When they got to Wanderer Springs they found that Dr. Vestal had been called out of town. Over near Medicine Hill folks thought, expected to be gone all day. Polly was too sick to wait for his return, so they started for Medicine Hill, sending word ahead by fourteen-year-old Buster Bryant who volunteered to ride with the message.

It was August and the sun was hot and Polly cried out at every bump, so Edna stood and held a quilt to shade her, and Grover drove the mules as fast as he dared for Medicine Hill. They met Buster coming back. He had missed Dr. Vestal who was on his way to Bull Valley. Grover turned the mules towards Bull Valley with Buster racing ahead. Somewhere along that road, Grover stopped to kill a rattlesnake that was so big when it coiled it reached the hub of the wagon wheel. Polly was dying, but Grover was a father and there were other children to think of.

Dr. Vestal had left Bull Valley for Red Top. Buster rode to head off the wagon, telling Grover to go home. He would find Dr. Vestal and meet them there. The mules had played out and Grover was walking beside them to lighten the load. Edna was standing with her feet spread, holding the stout little girl in her arms, trying to absorb the bumps and shocks of the wagon with her own body.

It was almost dark when the wagon got back home and Buster and the doctor were waiting. Edna was sitting beside Grover holding the child so that she lay across both their laps. The mules stopped of their own accord and neither Grover nor Edna made a move to get down. Dr. Vestal started to the wagon but Grover said, "I don't want you to touch her. We've been praying for you all day and listening to her die. I know it ain't your fault, but I don't want to see you now."

Grover got down, lifted Polly, and followed by Edna he

started towards the house. "Are you sure, Grover?" Dr. Vestal asked.

"She's not screaming any more is she?" Grover said. "I'd rather have her dead than have to listen to that."

Dr. Vestal left but Buster stayed with the Turrills, although he didn't dare go in the house. He unhitched the mules and fed them and sat on the graceless porch. After a while Grover came out to water the single tree in the yard, a stunted, ugly pear tree that Edna had planted and watered until it had finally dropped a few sun-baked pears as warty as horseapples.

Grover sat on the porch and stared out at the empty, treeless miles over which he had ridden that day, listening to the shriek of the wagon wheels and the dying cries of his last child.

After a while Edna came out also and leaned against the porch post, hugging the porch post as though it were a child, her head hanging down a little as though permanently bent from ironing clothes and chopping cotton. She waited while the last light of day faded and one by one the stars came out, watching the prairie that under moonlight had a sheen like a silent sea.

"If that cow hadn't died we'd be in California," Grover said.

"Old Boss," Edna said, remembering the name over all the years, recalling the dreams they had as they traveled across the prairie in the wagon.

"Damn country. Washes away every time it rains. Blows away every time there's a wind. Hail or grasshoppers every year. I've sweated over it. I've broken my back. It has taken every thing I have and given me nothing."

"Yeah," Edna said, looking out over the miles and years they had traveled together. "But ain't it purty."

Grover, whose eyes had darkened but not dimmed, nodded his agreement.

PICTURES

Amy Pruitt stole a glance at the clock. Ten minutes until five. The store was empty and Amy knew from experience that no one would come rushing in at the last minute to buy shoes or a dress. Not even on Friday or Saturday, and this was Tuesday. Still she sat at her little desk at the rear of her store, picking up bills, looking at them, and putting them down. She was in no hurry.

Amy was at that point in her forties when she tortured herself to slow the passage of time, aware that tomorrow was slipping away. She wasn't old, widows just seemed older than women who had their husbands and children and grandchildren about them. Widows had to work harder at being interesting and alive. She touched up her hair from time to time with a dark rinse so as not to appear too gray, and used makeup to soften the lines of her face. It was a strong, angular face and time had softened it, mellowed it, so that some people thought her prettier now than she had ever been.

Time had been kind in that respect. Her face did not sag and wrinkle the way the baby-faced ones did. She could remember when Cora Ledbetter had been class sweetheart, and everyone called her "Peaches" because of her round, pink face. That was when they were classmates, before they had both gotten married and remained in Wanderer Springs. The others had left and never returned. They'd probably call Cora "prunes" now. If they saw her. Amy wondered what they would call her.

They would think she still dressed nicely, Amy was sure of that. She got her clothes at the store. Some days she was the only customer. She usually wore a plain dark suit to work, and added a bit of color at the neck and wrists. A suit gave strength to her form, and the color added youth and femininity. She always wore high heel shoes in the store, even though her feet hurt, despising working class shoes. Once at a school outing she and the others had gone wading in a shallow creek after a picnic, her tiny white feet flashing in the clear water. "Your feet look like minnows," Roy had said. She remembered how funny it had sounded, and how delighted she had been. But her feet were not lovely now. More than anything about her, her feet looked old.

Amy took a long look at the clock, cleaned off her desk, slipped into her coat, set her chin, marched to the door, and turned the sign around, resolute in surrender. There had not been a single customer. Sometimes she wondered why she kept the store open. It barely made enough to pay the taxes. "We're going to have to close the store one of these days," Roy used to tell her. "You might as well make up your mind to it, we're going to have to move to some bigger town."

But she hadn't wanted to move. It had been her father's store; she had practically been reared there and had played hide-and-seek among the dresses and "let's pretend" with the shoes. The store had provided well for them then. She loved to be in the store on Saturdays when the farmers came to town to shop. Sometimes she met people who got off the train and came to the store to pass the time, people from curious places like Alabama and, one time, a man who claimed he was from New York. But the train didn't stop any more and the roads were so good the farmers drove to Center Point so they could leave the kids at the picture show while they shopped.

Amy took a final look at the store before closing and locking the door. She stood for a moment in the fading sunlight, feeling the biting wind. In Wanderer Springs there was always a wind. In the summer the hot wind parched her fair skin, in the winter it chafed it. I believe I'll go by the post office again, Amy thought. Maybe there's a letter from Jamie. It's been two weeks.

She walked past the Live and Let Live Grocery, its windows crammed full of goods without order or arrangement. She didn't look but she knew Biddy Whatley was sitting at the cash register commenting on everyone who passed. "I believe Amy Pruitt's putting on a little weight. Have you ever seen anyone age the way she has lately?"

She saw Orval Shipp coming out of the store and walked a little faster. Once, while pretending sympathy, he had pinched her arm. Old coot, and his wife as nice as she can be. She had dated Orval in high school and he hadn't been like that. That was when she had been a Percival.

She stopped beside the highway that ran through the

center of town. The speeding cars seldom slowed, as though the town were a mere nuisance in their path. Roy had, while crossing the street in this spot, been run over by a California motorist who sat in his car until the town constable arrived, not even bothering to look at the face of the man he had killed; not wanting to remember him, or the town, or the widow and fatherless child he had left in Texas.

Amy had gotten the man's name from the constable and had written him a letter. It hadn't been ugly or mean. She had just wanted the man to know what Roy was like. His folks had been sharecroppers and had to leave during the depression, but Roy had stayed and worked for her father, stocking, delivering packages, sweeping, and learning alterations. Roy was older than she and for a long time pretended he didn't notice her, but Roy was the only beau she ever had. Oh, she had dated Orval Shipp and like that, but they were just boys that she went with to high school things where Roy felt out of place. The night she graduated from high school she told her folks she aimed to marry Roy Pruitt, and her father said, "Well, he knows the store."

The man who ran over Roy didn't even answer her letter. She wasn't trying to make him feel bad, she just wanted to give him a picture of what Roy was like, what all of them were like. The man acted as though they ceased to exist the moment he was out of town. They don't care, Amy thought. They drive through town like we don't matter; just one more inconvenience in their way.

Seeing an opening in the traffic, Amy walked across the street, neither looking at the approaching cars nor hurrying her steps. This was her town and Amy Percival Pruitt was not going to dash across the street to avoid being run down by some stranger.

Inside the Post Office she paused to let her eyes adjust to the darkness, then walked to Box 6 and peered into the little glass window. The box was empty, not even a magazine, but she opened it any way, because once when she thought it was empty, she had found a card from Jamie lying unobserved in the bottom of the box. Standing on tiptoe, she looked into the open door and drew the tips of two fingers over the lip of the box. She dropped back on her heels, and firmly closed the box, making sure it was locked. She smiled to herself at how forgetful sons were, how many hours of grief they caused their mothers because of it.

Outside the Post Office she turned up her collar against the wind. It was still more than an hour before supper. Supper at the Traveler's Rest was always at 6:30, except on Sundays when it was early so Cora Ledbetter could go to church. Perhaps she should write Jamie more often. Perhaps he didn't understand how important his letters were to her. She wouldn't chide him, she would just tell him he might want to look at the new suits at the store, and who she saw, who asked about him. He was important to the town. Folks wanted to see him, to know how he was doing.

I think I'll go by the drugstore and have a cup of tea, she thought. Maybe Ginger has stopped at the drugstore before going home. Maybe she's heard from her son. Ginger's son had some kind of government job. He didn't write more regularly than Jamie, but he was always sending Ginger government pamphlets about such interesting things—pesticides, soil erosion, algae, water conservation.

Nora should remind Jamie. It was part of a daughter-in-law's responsibility. Nora was a good woman but severe, with definite plans of how her life would be. How their life would be. Nora knew how important little remembrances were. "She's a woman." Amy realized she was talking out loud and looked around to see if anyone heard her. Jamie was so busy being a husband and getting started in a career that he had little time to remember Wanderer Springs, to think of her. Nora should remind him.

She wondered if Jamie remembered Nora's birthday or their anniversary. She probably reminds him of those, she thought, then reprimanded herself. I mustn't be bitter towards Nora. I mustn't try to hold on to Jamie. He is a man now, old enough to have children of his own.

That was the one consolation of Jamie's marriage. Ever since Jamie's father had died, she had tried not to hold Jamie too tightly; she knew that some day she must give him up. She had sold her father's house so Jamie could go to college, even though she knew he might never return. When Jamie told her about Nora, a Dallas girl with aspirations, she kept telling herself, "There will be grandchildren. You are losing a son, but there will be grandchildren. They will come for Christmas and a week in the summer." But there were no grandchildren, and Nora didn't feel comfortable visiting in Wanderer Springs although Amy arranged for them to have a room of their own at the boarding house. Nora said Wanderer Springs was "a backwater." Which was not true. How could they be a backwater when there was a coast-to-coast highway running right through the middle of town. Besides, she kept up with things and lots of other folks did too.

Amy could not see into The Corner Drug because the front window was filled with colorful signs announcing a new bunion remover, a revival at the Baptist Church, the Wanderer Springs basketball tournament, and a high school victory dance. She opened the door and strange faces turned to look at her, a row of smiling faces like endless reflections in a mirror. "There's a seat here," one of them said.

She stepped back and let the door close. Strangers having a cup of coffee before the basketball tournament. It wasn't that she was unneighborly, it was just that strangers were too loud, too eager to be noticed, too determined not to fit in.

She walked east along the highway, her heels turning awkwardly, the gravel bruising her feet through the thin soles. She turned down the unmarked dirt street, catching the full fury of the wind on her back, walked past the uninhabited gingerbread house that was falling to ruin, the brick ranch-style house with the redwood fence that had been for sale for more than a year, the fading gray and yellow frame, and turned down the flagstone walk of The Traveler's Rest.

Despite its name, The Traveler's Rest was occupied solely by townspeople. The rooms were rented on a monthly basis and the roomers took their meals there. When Amy first came to The Traveler's Rest, after she had sold her house, all the rooms had been occupied. Since then, Mr. Baskin had died of a blood clot, Mrs. Gordon had gone to live with her children in Arizona, Mr. Clendon, who had started wandering away from the house and getting lost, had been placed in the state hospital in Wichita Falls, and Clo had died in her room with Amy holding her hand. Now, Amy and Mrs. Walsh were the only roomers the Ledbetters had and Mrs. Walsh was from Truscott. Amy couldn't imagine why she was living in Wanderer Springs. For a time Mrs. Walsh had lived across the hall from Amy, but when the room became available downstairs, Mrs. Walsh moved so she wouldn't have to climb the stairs.

Amy no longer looked at the house with its ugly, broken outline against the treeless sky. The square, high-walled lower floor appeared to have exploded producing a second story that was all odd angles and gables, small narrow windows, and wasted spaces. She hated the house because the television antenna buckled in the middle, and because the third step on the veranda always gave as though it were going to snap under her weight, and because Charlie Ledbetter always came and opened the door for her. He always smiled at her as though he had some special knowledge of her because they lived in the same house and ate at the same table. And because of his theory about widows.

Amy did not look at the maroon rug with yellow and blue flowers that ran up the stairs and down the hall and had the odor of dust and rot. She climbed the stairs to her room as though they separated her from all that was interesting and alive. She opened the door to her room, which was never locked, and flipped the light switch. It was the upstairs corner room with two windows, but one was small and crowded into a gable and the other one, though larger, was recessed between two angles of the ceiling. Even in summer the room was dim and she needed a light to read by. After lighting the gas heater and standing beside it for a moment to get the chill from her bones, she took off her coat, removed her high heel shoes, and slipped into her warm, comfortable bedroom slippers. Standing close to the heater for warmth, she pulled off her suit and shook it out and brushed it before hanging it in the closet. Then she put away her coat and shoes and looked at the clock.

There was too much time to do nothing, yet not enough time to start anything before supper. If she had a letter it would be different. It took time to read a letter; to read it for news, and then to reread it for memories. She read of the parties and games that Jamie and Nora went to, the movies they saw, the people they met; all the interesting things they did, and she stored them away with her memories, so that after a while, she too became a part of their lives. Once Mrs. Walsh had remarked on how long it took her to read a letter. "There is no correct way to read a letter," she replied.

Tonight there was not anything to look forward to, for after supper she would climb the stairs to her room and read or sew or listen to the radio until she could go to sleep. Sometimes she sat in the parlor downstairs and watched television with Charlie Ledbetter and Mrs. Walsh, but they had to watch the shows that Charlie chose and he liked shows that portrayed men as always strong and often vicious, and women as always helpless and often stupid, and that were set in cities that were always corrupt and often debased. Worse, he made comments on the programs as though they were real. There was nothing tonight that she would watch.

She slipped on a warm housecoat and rode her stationary bicycle for fifteen minutes, then did thirty sit-ups. Because she was not tall, she had always had to watch her weight, and this was particularly true now. After finishing her exercises, she went down the hall to shower, then put on a pretty but comfortable housedress and made her face. What would she talk about during supper?

Mrs. Walsh never left the house, never had company, enjoyed nothing but food, read only detective stories, and knew nothing of art, nature, or conversation. She didn't converse, she catalogued complaints. The house was too hot, the house was too cold, the food was tasteless, the linoleum in her room was worn, or broken, or ugly. Nothing interested her but complaints, symptoms, brutal crimes, and viruses.

Cora Ledbetter had always been short, and plain faced. She had resigned herself to never being attractive, and instead became busy and gay. That's how she got to be class sweetheart and nicknamed Peaches. It also had earned her a husband, a boarding house, presidency of the Women's Missionary Society, and she seemed confident that it would keep them, although she had gotten prune faced and dumpy.

Amy and Cora had always been friends although Amy had never entirely forgiven Cora for smiling and waving from her car during Roy's funeral procession. As the procession passed down Main Street, Cora saw someone from her Sunday School class and smiled and waved. Amy tried to tell herself it had been spontaneous, that Cora had acted without thinking; still it wasn't the way to behave. Besides, Cora always acted like she was still running for class sweetheart.

A childless woman, Cora had adopted her boarders. She told them the price of everything they ate and recited the recipe, she told anecdotes about former boarders and how they had died, gossiped about her Sunday School class, and kept them informed as to the schemes and machinations of four soap operas. Sometimes Amy couldn't tell the plots in the soap operas from those in the Sunday School class.

Charlie Ledbetter was a large, slow moving, slow talking handyman with large, blunt hands and small puffy feet. He always dressed in khaki pants and khaki shirt, the shirt faded and frayed, the trousers creaseless, with the fly forced open at the belt by his increasing paunch, and the zipper suspended carelessly half way down the track. In the house he kept his shoe laces untied in order to ease his puffy feet. At meals he loosened his belt in order to stuff himself with ease.

Charlie imagined flirtations and seductions in every house he visited to unstop a drain or repair a leaky faucet. He lorded it over the women in his house like an old lover; meddling in their affairs, teasing them unmercifully, and telling them stupid lies about lonely widows and spinsters who called him pretending they had a job for him to do. Most galling of all, he believed, actually believed, that Amy dressed to catch his eye, and that all her efforts to preserve decorum were affectations to tease him.

She had never understood why Cora had married that man. Of course there hadn't been many boys to choose from and Charlie had been on the football team and vice president of the Future Farmers of America, but his folks had never had anything except the house that he turned into The Traveler's Rest. Even in high school Charlie had been slack, and now the best part of his life was looking. Not like Roy. Roy had been a doer. Roy had made something of himself.

Amy looked at the photograph of Roy that she kept on the dresser. It was her favorite memory of her husband. He was standing in front of the store, dressed in a dark suit the way he always was when he opened the door. He took off his coat to sweep or make alterations, but he was always in a suit when he opened the door. In the photograph, on the other side of the door, was nine-year-old Jamie, also dressed in a dark suit. Between them they held the sign that signified her father's store was open. Amy thanked God that she had had that portrait made of the men in her life. Roy was killed a few days later and buried in the suit he was wearing in the photograph.

Amy sat in the chair beside the floor lamp and looked at her current magazines. In addition to *Time* and *Newsweek*, she subscribed to *Saturday Review*. Few of the movies and none of the books or plays mentioned in *SR* ever got to Wanderer Springs, or even Center Point, but Amy wanted to know what Jamie and Nora were reading and seeing. She never mentioned the books or movies at supper, not after Charlie had suggested she was interested in them for titillation, but she did try to talk about something besides local gossip. She tried to talk about concerns they had in common with other folks, other towns.

Time had an article on hunger, but she didn't want to bring that up again because Charlie believed hunger was synonymous with black people, and the last time she had mentioned it, he had said "nigger" until she cried.

Newsweek had a story on working women, but Charlie believed a woman's place was in the home, and that included widows. Cora forgave Amy for working, but believed working mothers were the direct cause of teenage pregnancies. Amy remembered Cora when she was sixteen and Cora hadn't been a Baptist then.

Amy was fascinated by the space program and loved to read and talk about the astronauts, but Cora quoted Bible verses and said God didn't want man in space, and Charlie talked about how much it cost. Charlie had always been cheap. He had taken Cora to Center Point to a movie for their honeymoon.

She didn't dare mention crime or Mrs. Walsh would tell again about some phantom sniper in Texarkana and how terrified she was of him although that had been more than twenty years and three hundred miles away.

Tonight she was going to talk about water. She could remember artesian wells, a time when there were springs all over the county, springs that were now dry. *Time* said it was a growing problem for the whole country. The last time she had tried to talk about it, Charlie had seen it as an excuse for him to talk about how much water the women wasted with bathing and washing their hair, and Cora said if Charlie washed his hair more often it wouldn't have that sour milk smell and that was probably why he was going bald, and Mrs. Walsh said she didn't take a bath or wash her hair because the bathroom was drafty and the hall was like ice.

It was never conversation. That was what she minded most about being alone—having no one to share with, no one who expanded her horizons, who broadened her thoughts. That's why she treasured Jamie's letters. He was her link to life.

"Amy," Cora Ledbetter called from downstairs.

"I'll be right down," Amy said, thinking her watch was slow.

"Charlie and I won't be here for supper. Charlie's sister is sick and we have to go over and stay with her for a while. I hope you don't mind being alone."

"No, of course not."

"Mrs. Walsh is having supper in her room. Would you like me to bring you a tray?"

"That would be fine," Amy said, but it wasn't. Eating with Charlie Ledbetter who pushed his food with his fingers and wiped his mouth with his handkerchief was better than eating alone. Why else would Cora have married him?

Although she was eating alone, Amy remained dressed. Eating in a housecoat was perhaps more comfortable but it was the kind of comfort that led to slovenliness and then to senility. Reading while eating made the evening run together without occasion.

Amy believed that time collapsed upon itself. First the years ran together, then the seasons seemed the same, then weeks passed without differentiation. When one's day became a seamless garment, the garment quickly faded to gray and life, at least conscious life, was over. She would not allow the evening meal to fade into bedtime reading. Rather, she would entertain herself with pleasant scenes from the past.

While she ate she recalled how Jamie had manfully fought back tears of disappointment when he opened his birthday present and found a book satchel instead of the toy horse he wanted, and then his tears of happiness when he opened the satchel and found the toy horse inside. Amy laughed the way she had then. She remembered the red Big Chief tablet he had placed in the satchel for his first day of school. She remembered the way Roy had looked at his son the first time, surprised, and proud, and slightly repelled at the rawness of birth. She remembered the way Jamie had stood beside his father's grave with the same look—surprised, proud, repelled at the rawness of death.

Those were her treasures but she had no one with whom to share them. She picked at her food then pushed the tray aside. She could remain dressed and go downstairs and watch any television program she wanted, just sit and let the words and images wash over her until time for bed. No, that was too comfortable. She would get a book and read herself to sleep.

She was looking at the books on the bedside table when she heard a knocking on the front door. Charlie had locked himself out. And Mrs. Walsh wouldn't get up at night for anybody. She could imagine Mrs. Walsh with her ear at the door, wanting to know what was going on without being a part of anything.

She opened the front door upon a young man her son's age who stood with his shoulders hunched against the cold. "You got a room for the night?" he asked briskly, his breath vaporizing in the air.

"I beg your pardon?"

"I'd like a room for the night."

"This is a boarding house," she said. "The rooms are let by the month."

"Look, I got to sleep somewhere. Give me a cot in the hall or I'll have to sleep out there," he said, jerking his head towards a large diesel tractor and trailer parked in the street.

"You'll have to talk to Mrs. Ledbetter. I just room here."

"Okay, let me talk to her," he said irritably.

"She's not here just now."

He stood on the exposed veranda, his hands thrust deep into his trouser pockets, his head bowed, not in resignation or defeat, but in suppressed anger. She knew what he was thinking, that they were backward, even stupid. The wind whipped the upturned collar of his leather jacket.

"I guess you can come in and wait," she said.

"If you don't mind," he said sarcastically. "I thought you were going to let me freeze to death on the front porch."

"May I ask your name?"

"Bruce," he said. "Sidlinger."

There was still a bite to his tongue, but what an unusual

name. She had never heard that name in this county. "I'm Mrs. Pruitt. This is our parlor, Mr. Sidlinger. You can wait here until Mrs. Ledbetter returns."

"Thanks." He made no effort to stifle a yawn as he sprawled on the couch and unzipped his jacket.

The gesture was so boyish that she smiled, thinking of her son. The thought of Mrs. Walsh starting down the hall to the bathroom and being startled by a strange young man in the parlor prevented her from leaving. I invited him in, I am responsible for entertaining him until Cora returns, she thought. She sat in the chair across from him.

"How did you come to stop here? There's no sign . . ."

"Everything was full in Center Point. They said this was the closest place. I haven't stopped since North Carolina. I may go to sleep sitting here."

"Are you from North Carolina?"

"I'm not from nowhere. The east mostly, but I've been everywhere. I've never been through here before."

She noted that he said "through here" as though her town were an obstacle, a—a hazard he had to pass through. "Where is your family? Your mother? Surely you have a mother?"

"Last I heard she was in some Podunkville in Pennsylvania."

"Don't you write her? Call her? She must be worried sick about you."

He had been half-reclining, his close-cropped head on the back of the couch, his eyes half-closed. At her question, he straightened a little and leveled his head to look at her.

His nose was not broad but there was a broad space between his eyes, and one eye seemed to be slightly larger and higher than the other, giving him a quizzical expression. He skewed one side of his mouth before he spoke. "It's as safe as you make it," he said. "Drunk drivers and hitchhikers. But I figure the main danger is hitchhikers. They hang out at truck stops. One time a girl asked me for a ride to California so she could marry her boyfriend. She was willing to pay for it, too. She was running away from home because her folks wouldn't let her get married."

"Did you give her a ride?"

"Hell no, I don't want to get mixed up in someone else's problems. I don't never pick up hitchhikers."

A desperate girl trying to reach the man she loved—perhaps it was wise not to help her against her parents' wishes. But surely there were others—surely there were some he had helped. "I bet you've been all over this land." She saw the open road running long and broad before her, leading the way to new places, new people, to mountains, valleys, rivers, and great sprawling cities. "You have seen so much."

"You got that right. I been in a million towns like this one. Dirty cafes, cheap motels, all night restaurants, truck stops. I've seen it all."

She was caught off guard at his view of his life. "But you must have met many wonderful people."

"Yeah. A couple of hundred waitresses. A couple of thousand gas station attendants. A hundred loading crews. A dozen cops. It adds up. To a big fat nothing."

Her life, too, was like that. "All our lives are like that," she said. "Meeting people but never touching. I wonder what happened to them, all those people I have met but never known. My customers. My senior class. Mrs. Walsh. Hundreds of people pass through this town every day. Most don't even stop, don't even slow down. They don't even know the name of our town. They pass through as though the lives we live here are something apart from their lives. And we live our lives as though those who pass up and down the highway are an intrusion. As though their joy and sorrow were not a part of our own. We are all strangers. We should hold out our hands to each other."

She was warmed by the compassion that reached out to all the world, that extended particularly to the homeless travelers who followed a strip of concrete, their lives no broader than the hard, narrow trail they followed, speeding down the main streets of country towns, sending dust and children scattering, until they were swallowed up in the vast loneliness of the country.

"Haven't you often wished as you passed through towns like this that there were someone who cared? Someone who reached out to you? Mr. Sidlinger? Mr. Sidlinger, are you asleep?"

"Sorry. I must have dozed off."

"I'm afraid I've been babbling."

"That's okay," he said, stretching and yawning.

She knew that in his eyes she was a woman who had never been anywhere or seen anything, but she had seen something very clearly and it was important that he see it too. "I was just saying what a wonderful chance you have to travel all over the country and meet all kinds of people. Isn't that more important than getting from one place to the next as quickly as possible?"

"I get paid by the load. The sooner I deliver this one, the sooner I get started on the next."

"But all these years on the road will mean nothing if you have no picture of the country and the kind of people we are." She could see he didn't understand what she was talking about. "Isn't it strange that you and I have met like this? By accident. And isn't it wonderful? You are from nowhere and have been everywhere, and I have lived my entire life in this place. Yet, we have met, and we have shared a . . ." Was vision too grand a word? ". . . an understanding. We will never meet again, but I will remember you wherever you are, and wherever you are, you will know that I am here and that I care."

"Yeah, well. . . . Do you think it would be all right if I just stretched out here on the couch? I'm bushed, and this sitting around talking is costing me money."

She didn't know what to say. She was sure Charlie would welcome the chance to make a few dollars, but she had no authority to let a room. "I suppose I could tell Mrs. Walsh and leave Mr. Ledbetter a note. . . ."

"I'd be obliged."

"Mrs. Walsh," she said, tapping lightly on the door. "Mrs. Walsh."

"What do you want?" The door did not open.

"There is a young man who is going to spend the night

here. I'm leaving Mr. Ledbetter a note."

The door opened slightly and Mrs. Walsh stuck out her head to look at the young man. "This house is for people who live here," she said, and retreated inside her room, firmly closing the door and locking it.

Amy turned to apologize to Mr. Sidlinger but getting to bed seemed to be his only concern. She wrote a note to Charlie Ledbetter explaining that she was allowing a young man to spend the night and that he had agreed to pay whatever was reasonable. She wondered if she should warn Mr. Sidlinger that Charlie would try to overcharge him?

"I'm afraid there aren't any sheets on the bed," she said, leading him upstairs. She stopped at the hall closet to get blankets before showing him the cold, damp room.

"Just give me the blankets," he said, lighting the small gas heater. "It's cold as hell in here."

She helped him make the bed. When they were finished, she paused, reluctant to say goodnight. There were so many things she wanted to tell him. "A person can't live to himself," she said, trying to compress it into something he could remember. "Not all the time."

He stood, staring at the floor, considering.

She hoped he wasn't staring at her feet; she was in her house shoes and her feet made her look so old. She bobbed her head and smiled to shift his attention to her face. "To be alive you must open yourself to other people."

He zipped up his leather jacket and hugged himself, turning his back to the fire.

"You may come to my room until yours gets warm if

you'd like," she offered.

"Uh, thanks. I'm sorry to do this to you but I'm really tired. No offense, I've just been on the road too long."

She knew that he thought she was an old and dull woman who knew nothing worth hearing, but it wasn't true. She had so much to say if only there were someone to listen. "I hope I haven't bored you," she said. "I just wanted you to have a picture of what we are like."

"Maybe after I've had a couple hours of sleep," he said. "I'd like to, but right now I'm bushed. Maybe I could stop by your room on my way out." He squeezed her arm to make his intentions clear.

She was shocked at the person who stood before her. A stranger. A perfect stranger. She blinked at him, seeing him for the first time. A brute. Too stunned to speak, to think, she slowly backed from the room, feeling behind her for the door. She fled to her room, closing and locking the door. Too agitated to sit, she tried to think what she should do. The arrogance. The stupidity. She'd march to his room and tell him he was vulgar. A common—knock on his door and demand an apology. Knock on his door and—she couldn't face him. She knew if he was there in the morning she would have to move even if she had to go to Center Point to find a place to stay.

But could she allow him to think what he did of her and people like her in towns like this? She would write a note and slip it under his door. But what would she say? And what if he opened the door as she was leaving the note? She could explain to Cora and let Cora tell him. But she couldn't face Cora Ledbetter, and besides, Cora would tell Charlie and she couldn't endure that. She couldn't. Too agitated to sit, she paced the room, biting a knuckle, thinking of leaving the town that had been her home all her life.

She would go to bed. When she got up the next morning, he would be gone. No one would ever know. No one except Bruce Sidlinger riding around the country with that picture of her in his mind. For a moment she thought she couldn't bear it. She had lived a modest and circumspect life. There was not a trace of gossip about her. How could she bear the thought. . . . She wouldn't think about it. She wouldn't think about him either. He would never come this way again, why should she think of him?

She started to undress. What she needed was a hot bath. Suddenly she realized that the bathroom was no longer hers but theirs. She had lived upstairs so long alone that she had begun thinking that the bathroom was hers. She even acted like it, leaving personal items, soap, towel, toothbrush, deodorant in the bathroom. The rinse she used on her hair. Her secrets were open to that swine. A horrid thought came to her. She had not gotten a towel or wash cloth for him. What if he used her soap, her wash cloth? For a moment she cried because she was lonely, and humiliated, and because nothing belonged to her anymore.

Then she was angry. How dare he? How dare he come into her life like that and take over the bathroom, take over the entire upstairs, the whole house with his presence? She had tried to be a person to him, but he was too stupid to understand. Stupid lout. She hated him.

She went to bed but she did not sleep. She heard the Ledbetters return around midnight. She heard the wind die shortly before dawn. She heard Mr. Sidlinger moving around in his room. She heard him leave his room and walk down the hall. He stopped outside her door and tried to open it. He knocked softly on the door. "It's me," he said. "You awake?" He couldn't even remember her name.

He knocked again. Louder this time. She was afraid he would wake the others. She wanted to yell at him to go away. She wanted to open the door, tell him what she thought of him and others like him, and slam the door in his face. She pulled the covers tightly around her and cringed in her bed.

"Wake up. I'm going to have to go soon." He scratched at the door like a dog. She could hear him impatiently shifting his feet. "Are you going to open the door or not?" He rattled the door knob. She was certain she could hear someone downstairs. He rattled the door again. "Bitch," he said. She could hear the stairs creaking under his weight and voices below.

She cried again and then for the first time all night fell soundly asleep.

"Amy, breakfast is ready. We're waiting for you," Mrs. Ledbetter called.

"I'll be right down," she answered. Mechanically she got out of bed and went to the bathroom to wash. She inspected the soap and towel. The wash cloth felt suspiciously damp. She splashed water on her face and went back to her room to dry. She dressed, carelessly putting on the suit she had worn the day before. When she reached the dining room, breakfast was in progress.

"You overslept this morning," Charlie Ledbetter said, as though it were a victory for him.

"I didn't sleep well last night."

"No wonder, as cold as it was," said Mrs. Walsh. She was dressed in a heavy man's robe, the pockets bulging with tissues. "And with that man upstairs," she hissed.

Amy could not look at them.

"Here, you have some hot coffee. It'll make you feel better," Cora said.

"Thank you," she said, provoked almost to tears by the simple kindness. "I don't think I'll have any breakfast. I'll just drink my coffee and go on to work. I'm running a little late this morning."

"So Amy Pruitt spent the night upstairs with a man," Charlie said.

"Charlie," Cora admonished. "You're embarrassing Amy."

"I wouldn't have slept one minute if I'd known he was in the house," Mrs. Walsh said.

"I told you he was staying," Amy said, flabbergasted.

"Picked up a nice piece of change," Charlie said. "I think I'll put a sign out on the highway. I could probably get somebody two, three times a week."

"I'll move," Amy said. "I vow I will. I'll move to Center Point."

They all looked at her in surprise. "I didn't know you minded," Cora said.

"You let him in," Charlie said. "You told him he could stay. He left a message for you," Charlie said.

"Who?"

"Your friend. That guy slept upstairs."

Amy could feel the heat rise to her face. She was so edgy this morning, so out of sorts she felt she was going to cry. Why were they so cruel?

"Don't you want to know what he said?" Charlie persisted.

She didn't. She truly didn't. She wished she had never seen him. She wished she didn't know such people existed.

"He said for me to tell you, 'Thanks for the picture.' "

"What does that mean?" Cora asked.

"Did you give him a picture of yourself?" Mrs. Walsh said, opening her mouth and eyes in a caricature of surprise.

"Of course not."

"Then why did he say that?"

"If you'll excuse me, I must get ready for work," Amy said, rising from the table. She had her foot on the stairs when Cora caught up with her.

"Don't pay any attention to Charlie. He just has to have his fun."

Although she tried to will it back, Amy could feel a tear trickling down her cheek.

"Why don't you take the day off and stay in your room and rest?" Cora said. "It's so bad out, and you don't feel well."

"I don't think I could bear to stay in all day," Amy said, surprising even herself. She hadn't meant to say it, but it was true. It was a relief to get to the store.

Once outside she felt better although it was bitterly cold and had begun to sleet. She knew she was ruining her good shoes, but what could she do? At the end of the street she turned and started walking in the gravel along the side of the highway. A car honked behind her but she did not turn.

"Hey, you want a ride?" someone shouted. "I'm going into town. It sure is a bad day for walking."

Out of the corner of her eye she saw a middle-aged man driving his car slowly abreast of her. His cheeks were pink from a close and recent shave, his hair too neatly trimmed, too carefully sprayed into place. A sign on the car identified it as belonging to a chain of restaurants, the kind that served breakfast all day.

She would like to ride. It was bitterly cold and the gravel hurt her feet. But she couldn't. It was up to her to show outsiders the kind of people who lived here. Proud, independent, and honorable. Yes, honorable. She lifted her chin.

"Come on, lady, you can't walk in weather like this."

Ahead of her she could see the store, her father's store. Defiantly she crossed the road without looking, ignoring the screech of tires and a loud honk, conscious of the picture she made. Amy Percival Pruitt did not dance for strangers. Dressed in a dark suit the way she always was, she unlocked the door and turned the sign so that it read "Open."

THE SAVIOUR OF THE BEES

The summer I was thirteen I was the saviour of the bees. At least that's what I called myself. Dad called me his little farmer, especially when he was pleased with the way I did my chores. Mother called me "Granddaddy Longlegs" because I was always hanging around thinking, and because I was all arms and legs and tall like her side of the family. Dad was dark and thick-shouldered and stocky. Mother once bought him a pair of high heeled cowboy boots to make him look taller but Dad wouldn't wear them. Dad had once been a cowboy but said he had outgrown it.

It was the third summer in a row my mother had planned a trip we did not take. The first had been to Fort Worth so I could see the zoo, the second to Carlsbad so I could see the caverns, the third to Corpus Christi because Mother wanted me to see the ocean.

Mother made careful plans and enlisted my support. "Tell your father that the other children have all seen the zoo." "Tell your father that your teacher went to Carlsbad Caverns and said it was something you should see." "Tell your father that you'd do better in Geography if you could see the ocean." I told him but we never got caught up enough with the farm work to be able to go.

It was the summer Dad gave Mother a new pressure

cooker for her birthday. Because of the war a lot of things were rationed, but we raised our own beef, pork, chickens, and had an orchard and a garden besides the field crops. The pressure cooker would make it easier for Mother to can fruits and vegetables for the winter. Dad said no matter what fool thing Roosevelt did we were self-sufficient.

Dad and I picked out the cooker and I distracted Mother while Dad hid it, and I placed it in the kitchen the night before her birthday, after he and Mother had gone to bed.

The morning of her birthday, Dad and I sat at the table passing looks, waiting to hear Mother's gasp of surprise when she discovered the cooker. I was trying not to laugh, and then Dad saw something that made his face change. I looked too. Mother was standing at the stove frying our eggs, and she was crying, the tears sizzling when they hit the hot skillet.

I thought Mother must be crying because Dad was sitting at the table in his low quarter shoes with no socks. Dad didn't wear socks in the summer time, not even to town, because they made his ankles hot. Mother said it made him look loose and spiritless. Mother was younger than Dad (she said he had married as an afterthought), and from the city where folks wore socks all year round and were Democrats.

"Why are you crying?" I asked her.

"It does seem to me that sometimes I could be something besides a farmhand," she said, speaking to Dad, not to me.

The wives of Dad's friends talked about how young and

pretty Mother was, but Mother didn't feel pretty. "Do you think my face is getting leathery?" she asked me sometimes. "Do you think my hair looks tired?" Now I knew what the words meant. Her eyes were puffy, her dark hair was damp and stringy. I noticed how hot and red her hands were, and the little lines around her mouth, and the way her shoulders sagged making her neck look long. Mother felt old.

"Maybe if I were one of your cows you'd appreciate me," she said to Dad, looking at him now, her eyes hard and angry. "Maybe you'd do nice things for me."

Dad did do nice things for his cows, and he had the look he had when Beulah tried to hook him when he picked up her new calf. Beulah was his favorite cow, the one he bragged on, and he wasn't so much angry, because a man had to expect that kind of thing from a cow, as puzzled and disappointed that it was Beulah, after all he had done for her.

"We got the pressure cooker to make things better for you," Dad said. "The man said it would save you lots of time."

"Time is all I have. All I do is work so what am I saving time for?" Mother asked. "We never go anywhere. We never do anything." Tears were still rolling down her face and her mouth was pinched and ugly. "Did you ever think that I might like something pretty?" She put the plates of bacon and eggs before us and left the room.

I remembered then how carefully she had shown me the rings, bracelets, watches, earrings in the catalog. "When you get married," she said, "these are the kinds of things you should give your wife." But I wasn't even thinking about getting married, and I was impatient to show her the .22

rifle I wanted for my birthday.

After Mother went into her room, closing the door, Dad and I ate quickly, wanting to be out of the house, and knowing there was a lot of work to do before we ate again. "I don't know what she wants," Dad said, taking his hat from the nail beside the door before he left the house. "I gave her the prettiest place in the county."

It was the summer Dad began sleeping in my room because he had to be up early and Mother stayed up late reading books she checked out of the county library. They were romances and mysteries, mostly. She said it was to fill up all the time the pressure cooker saved her.

I thought Dad was trying to make up to Mother because he spent so much time in the fields I was sure we would get caught up with the farm work and go to Corpus Christi. The only time he came in the house was when it was time to eat or go to bed.

He and Mother didn't talk much at the table any more, and when they did I wished they didn't. "Do you think you might get through today in time for me to go to town and get groceries?" Mother asked one morning. Her face had that stiff, tight look that made her eyes and mouth look small. The only time she could get books from the library was when we went to town to get groceries.

"What do we need from town?" Dad asked. His face was swollen. Dad had a short, thick neck, and when he was mad he didn't seem to have any neck at all. Dad didn't like the idea that Mother needed something he couldn't provide.

"Salt and sugar if I'm going to do any canning with the

pretty new pressure cooker you bought me."

I stayed away from the house as much as I could. When I finished my chores I went down to the corral and watched the bees trying to get water. I liked to watch the bees. They worked so hard. They had worn the opening to the hive smooth with their coming and going to the honeysuckle and lilac bushes Mother had planted to hide the wire fence that kept the chickens out of the yard. Mother said that people had to be removed from animals. "Decent distance," she called it.

I had never noticed how many bees drowned in the water tank. They scrambled around the sides of the tank, climbing over one another. When the cows stuck their muzzles in the water, the water came up over the bees and they floated around in little circles until they drowned. Wasps floated on top of the water like they thought they were gods.

One morning at the table I asked Dad why wasps floated while bees drowned. Dad knew everything about animals. He could just look at an animal and tell what was wrong with it and what it needed. "Bees have little hairs on their legs," he said. "That's how they gather pollen to make honey. The hairs break the surface tension of the water and they drown. Wasps don't have hairs because they don't make honey, so they can float."

"But that's not fair," I said, appalled that bees were doomed by the very thing that made them valuable, while wasps that did nothing but wound, floated on the water, safe because they didn't make honey or anything else that people could use. "Wasps don't do anything but make nests for themselves."

"Why did you have to tell him that?" Mother demanded. "You have to make everything so ugly."

Dad was not normally a violent man but he appeared about to explode. His neck had disappeared and his head was swollen. "Everything in life is not pretty," he said.

"When you're young it can be," Mother said. "For a little while."

Mother looked at me like she was going to read to me from the Bible. Mother didn't study the Bible the way some folks did, she read it for answers, the way others read the advice columns in the newspaper. And when she read it to me she took on a look that said, you don't have to understand this, you just have to believe that it is for the best.

"Jimmy," she said. Her voice was low and thoughtful, not the way she talked to Dad. "Jimmy, wouldn't you rather be a bee and make something beautiful like honey, even if it made you liable to drowning, than to be a wasp and be hated and feared by everybody?"

"What good is it telling him things like that?" Dad asked. "Bees don't have any choice in the matter, or wasps either."

"People do," Mother said. "We can choose whether we want to do something beautiful with our lives or just think of ourselves."

"Wasps make nests just like bees," Dad said, "and they defend them."

"They don't sacrifice their lives the way a bee does, because when a bee stings you it dies."

They had forgotten all about me and the bees, too. I slipped out of the house with Dad describing the difference between a bald, frayed-wing worker and a sleek and useless drone.

"I thought the drones were all males," Mother said.

I went down to the corral and dipped the bees out of the water. It wasn't fair that bees drowned and wasps floated, and the only thing I knew to do was put myself on the side of the bees.

I started making regular rounds each day, rescuing the bees, placing them on the corral fence to dry their wings, taking care not to be the cause of their self-destruction. It was frustrating saving the bees as they never seemed to learn. I took broken shingles from the barn and made little rafts for them to climb on while I was away at work. Sometimes I splashed water at the wasps trying to make them liable too, but they just flew away.

One day Mother came down to the tank and put her arm around me. She had on her Bible-reading face. "Jimmy, I'm going to leave your father," she said, "and I want you to go with me. Don't you want to go with me?"

She wanted me to look at her but I couldn't. I couldn't look at the house either because I knew Dad was watching. I just looked at the bees, drowning in the water.

"I don't want you to hate your father," she said. "He's a good man, he works hard, he loves this place. He likes plowing and taking care of the cattle. He doesn't want anything else. But there's so much more. Jimmy, if you stay here you'll be buried just like I am. You'll just be a farmhand taking care of his place, feeding his cattle, raising his crops. Come with me."

She waited for me to say something but I didn't. I couldn't. I couldn't get my breath.

"I'm going to the house to get my things," she said. "If you want to go with me, go to the car. Your father won't try to stop you."

I wasn't sure when she started to the house but I was sure when Dad was there beside me. I could feel him standing there, like at night when it was so dark I couldn't see the barn but I could feel it there, towering over me.

"I know your mother talked to you," he said, "but I don't want you to go. I don't want you to have hard feelings about your mother. She is a good woman and she loves you, but she doesn't love this place the way you and I do. She wants things for herself, things she can put back there in that room of hers with the big bed and the fancy dresser, and all her pretty things. I know she wants what she thinks is best for you, but she'll just smother you in prettiness."

They wanted me to choose, but I couldn't help one and hurt the other. After a while, Dad left too, went into the barn I guess. Then I heard Mother come out of the house and get in the car. I don't know what she was taking with her but it seemed like she slammed every door on the car. Then she got in and started it. I could hear the drone of the car for a long time after she left.

I thought about drowning myself in the tank. I thought about running away. I didn't know what to do. After a while

Dad told me he had to go to town for a while and took the truck.

It was almost dark when he came back and I had already started the milking. "Your mother and I decided to stay together until you're grown," was all he said. Then I heard Mother drive in and slam all the car doors again, and go into the house and start cooking supper. It wasn't until we sat down at the table that I realized that Dad had put on socks before going to town.

Dad's face wasn't swollen but his head seemed sunk down into his shoulders so that he didn't have a neck. He looked pleased with himself and ashamed at the same time. Mother looked pretty. She looked like she felt pretty, and she kept pushing at her hair to put life in it.

We talked about Corpus Christi, and the ocean, and seeing sharks, and picking up sea shells. Supper seemed to last a long time as they kept talking and talking. Dad said, "Jimmy, go on to bed, you're about to fall out of your chair. I'm going to stay up for a while."

Mother said to Dad, "Why don't you sleep in my room and that way you won't wake Jimmy up when you get up in the morning."

I don't know what happened after that but we didn't go to Corpus Christi that summer. We didn't go to Grand Canyon the next summer either. Mother planned it and talked about it, and I drove a tractor all summer. Mother said I did the work of a man. Dad said he might as well sleep in my room since we both had to get up early, and since Mother stayed up late reading.

I guess the bees took care of themselves. I didn't have any time that summer to save them. And when Dad bought a new cook stove for Mother's birthday I didn't help him pick it out. I didn't help him hide it either.

Champion of the World

Colin was fourteen the Christmas he got the boxing gloves. "I want you to know how to defend yourself," his father said. "Don't ever start a fight and don't ever run from one."

His father had been in fights when he was younger. Colin knew that. He also knew that his father had never run from one, not even when the other man had a stick. He had a scar over his eyebrow to prove it. Last year his father had fought a company that wanted to run power lines across the farm. Colin's mother said he might as well give in since he couldn't win, and he didn't win. His father said that wasn't the point.

"Keep your guard up," his father said, holding one of the gloves by the cuff and tapping Colin on the head with it. "And don't ever quit because you're behind."

The gloves were a deep royal purple, the color of ripe plums, and had white trim and laces. Colin pulled them on and they made his long, thin arms feel heavy and powerful. They also made him feel like hitting something, so he cuffed his sister until she cried and he was told to leave her alone. Playfully he punched his father on the shoulder, hoping his father would put on the other pair and spar with him, but his father was reading the paper and Colin was sent outside.

It was better out on the long, gray, rotting porch that sloped gently downward until it was buried in the dry brown tufts of bermuda grass that he could never reach with the lawn mower, and had never bothered to clip. From the porch he could still smell the Christmas cooking, but it was not stuffy like the kitchen, crowded with the tall, thin, nervous body of his mother who, carrying a fork in one hand, moved restlessly from the oven, to the gas refrigerator, to the table where his short, stout father had pushed aside the pans filled with pies and dressing to sit with his paper.

Colin stepped off the porch and walked around the side of the house that was showing signs of gray through the cracked and flaking white paint. He shadowboxed for a while and hit the house with a couple of left jabs, but it hurt his hand. He tried hitting the sagging wire fence that separated the yard and his mother's small but carefully tended flower bed from the scratching, pecking hens. The fence was loose and gave with the blows so that it didn't hurt his hands, but he ripped a three-cornered tear in his new gloves. For a moment, looking at the new gloves that were already marred, he wanted to cry. But fourteen-year-old boys didn't cry. Not boys who were going to be like Billy Conn. Not a boy who was going to be Champion of the World.

Colin shadowboxed, bobbing and weaving, his feet dancing the way he had seen at the picture show. Colin had never seen a fight except scuffling at school, but he had seen movies about boxers, and his father had taken him to the picture show to see films of prize fights. Colin knew what boxing was like.

Colin punished Joe Louis with sharp, stinging jabs, then knocked him down with a fast left-right, and cockily danced to a neutral corner, having dethroned the heavyweight champion of the world. Colin walked around with his arms raised in victory until the glory faded and he was left with no more worlds to conquer. He was tired of play-acting. He looked across the fields, old with bare, brown cotton stalks and tangled strips of dirty lint.

Colin liked living on the farm. He liked going to the pasture to hunt or fish or swim in the forbidden creek. He liked climbing the windmill to look for the cows, and sitting on the porch waiting for the stars to come out at the end of a summer day. He liked busting watermelons in the field and digging out the red, juicy meat with his hands. He didn't really mind the work. But a farm was a lonely place for a boy. He had no one to play with but Betty, his eight-year-old sister. Betty would throw the ball with him if he would push her in the tire swing, but they always ended up quarreling and his mother taking Betty's side.

Colin's father was always working. When the crops were laid by, he worked in the shop behind the garage, repairing the farm equipment, sharpening plow points, or planning barns or pens. When he was working in the shop, Colin's father liked to be left alone.

Colin started playing with Humps, the oldest of Wil-loliver's three children. Colin's father didn't like him to play with Humps. "Humps is a nigrah," he said. "He's not like you. If you can't find something to do, I'll find something for you." But there was no one else to play with, and he couldn't work all the time. His father didn't approve, but he didn't tell Colin not to.

Humps was the same age as Colin but larger, heavier. He was dark while Colin was light and badly freckled from the sun. Humps was stocky, heavily muscled, with smooth features and good teeth. Colin was slight and wiry, and had small eyes and nose and big ears and teeth.

Humps, who was named after his mother's birthplace, Humphrey, Texas, was a boy of many accomplishments. He could tell time by the trains that passed along the track about a mile away. Humps knew the schedule and destination of every train that passed. To Colin, a passing train was going to Wanderer Springs or Center Point, but to Humps every train went to St. Louis or Los Angeles, places of unparalleled wickedness and freedom. Humps always stopped to watch a train pass. "I declare," he'd say. "Seventeen minutes after ten. That's the Zephyr Eagle and she won't stop till she's in St. Louie."

Humps could make warts disappear, hypnotize horn toads, pop the heads off snakes, wring the necks of two chickens at one time, and fish with an old hook and a reel made by winding cord around a smooth bottle. These were specialties which Colin properly admired but never attempted. Colin's specialties were hunting, milking cows, driving a tractor, and throwing a football. Humps admired the .22 rifle and the football and stood in awe of cows and tractors.

Colin had been given the .22 for his twelfth birthday, to

teach him responsibility, and he used it to kill the jackrabbits that ate crops and the hawks that killed his mother's hens. Colin was expert with the rifle. When Colin went hunting he usually took Humps with him to flush rabbits out of the shinneries. When he killed a cottontail, he gave it to Humps to take home. Colin let Humps carry the rifle when they were out of sight of the house, but the one time he had offered to let Humps shoot the rifle, Humps had declined.

They swam together in the creek and worked side by side in the field, but they didn't compete to see who got to the end of the row first. Humps was content to work beside Colin or to run alongside him across the furrowed fields. When they wrestled and fell to ground, Humps stopped. It wasn't like he was giving up, it was like, for Humps, the game was over. Humps was stronger and when they were on their feet, he picked Colin up and tossed him around, but once they were on the ground he never tried to pin Colin, and Colin quickly got to his feet again.

Christmas Day was one of those windless winter days and although the ground was cold the sun was warm. Colin didn't want to go back inside. He looked across the brown fields to the pasture. He could get his rifle and go hunting, but he wanted to wear his new gloves. He went back into the house, unnoticed by his mother and father and his sister who was playing under the Christmas tree with her new doll. Colin pulled off the torn gloves, and took the other pair out of the box. Slipping those on, and carrying the torn pair under his arm, he passed through the yard, around the gray, tin topped barn that smelled of mice and corn, and down to the nigrah shack.

The nigrah shack was a three-room frame house standing on cedar posts. The house was dwarfed by tall cottonwood trees. The yard, bare and packed hard by the busy feet of children, was littered with their playthings—oval sardine cans wired together as make-believe trains, worn tires, the back seat of an automobile, and the rusting hulk of an old cultivator. Under the house were broken dishes, bundles of sticks tied together for brooms, and mason jar lids for making mud pies. A black family with three children lived in the small, solid rent-free house Colin's father provided so they would be available for work when he needed them.

The house was called the "nigrah shack" but it was not a shack. Although small, it was well built, in good condition, and newer than the house Colin lived in. The farm required periods of intense labor during hay and wheat harvesting and cotton chopping and picking. The house had been built to accommodate a family of workers. When Colin was small a white family had lived in the shack, but after Pearl Harbor all the white laborers had gotten jobs at Army bases or defense plants. Colin's father had to hire a black family. Willoliver had moved into the house with his wife, Madeline, two daughters, and Humps.

Humps was sitting in the open door of the porch-less shack. The smells of the wood stove, close bodies, and Christmas cooking poured out the open door. Humps was wearing a new red and green checked shirt and a green corduroy cap. Colin knew he had gotten them for Christmas. He walked up to the door, as was his right since his father owned the house. Humps and his family always stopped at the gate at Colin's house and waited to be invited into the yard. But Humps' family had no gate, no fence, no porch, and their door was open to the world.

"Christmas gift," Colin said.

"Christmas gift," Humps repeated.

Colin pulled Humps' cap over his eyes and Humps laughed, pleased that Colin had noticed.

"Them your gloves?" Humps asked.

"Yeah. Want to put them on?"

Humps pulled the gloves on his rough hands and stood up, pawing the air. "Man, that makes me feel like Joe Louis." Humps stalked about flat-footed, throwing great haymakers in the air.

Colin laughed. "That's not the way you box," Colin said. Colin knew. He had seen films of real boxing matches and Humps hadn't. Blacks couldn't go to the picture show, the drug store, the cafe, or the carnivals that came to town at harvest time. They had no sports equipment or playgrounds. They met behind the gin to run, wrestle, argue, and fight. Humps had been in fights during his rare trips to town, but they weren't boxing matches. All Humps knew about boxing was what he imagined about Jack Johnson and Joe Louis, blacks who had overcome the world. And what he had heard on the radio. Joe Louis and Billy Conn.

Willoliver had asked if he and Humps might listen to that fight. Colin's father had said yes and they had stood outside on the porch and Colin had turned the radio up loud so they could hear. The radio was on the refrigerator and

Colin stood in a chair so he could be close to it. His father sat across the room. No one spoke during the fight, but when Louis knocked Conn out, Colin could hear Humps jumping up and down in the yard.

Colin turned off the radio and stood on the chair watching his father who slowly got up to close the door. Willoliver, a short, heavy, prudent man, stood waiting, his worn hat held in his hands, to see if it was all right that Louis had won, as though he might be asked to take some of the blame. "Go on home," Colin's father said.

"Yes suh," Willoliver said.

"He's the champion of the world," Colin heard Humps say as Humps and his father passed through the gate on their way home. "That mean's there isn't no white man can whip him."

"Shut up, boy," Willoliver said.

"Don't it?" Humps said. "Don't it mean he is the best there is?"

"Shut up, boy," Willoliver said.

Colin had thought it absurd to think just because Joe Louis was champion of the world that he could whip any white man. Colin had asked his father and his father said that blacks had hard heads and that it was impossible to hurt one by hitting him in the head.

Colin laughed at Humps stalking about, his arms windmilling, imagining he was boxing. "You don't box like that," he said.

"Joe Louis do, and he's the champion of the world."

"That don't mean he can whip everybody," Colin said. "He hasn't fought everybody."

"Ain't nobody beat him yet."

"He ain't fought everybody yet."

"He beat Billy Conn."

Billy Conn was Colin's hero. He had often imagined himself Billy Conn as he danced around raining blows on the champion's head. Louis had knocked Conn out and Colin didn't have an answer for that.

Humps pulled the gloves off and held them in his hands admiring them. "Them sure are fine gloves," he said. "I aim to get me some like that."

"You don't swing your arms like this," Colin said, parodying Humps with head down, arms windmilling. "You punch straight, like this."

"I fight like Joe Louis do. You fight like Billy Conn."

Colin thought of teaching Humps to box. His father wouldn't like him teaching a nigrah to fight, but the gloves weren't much of a gift it he couldn't use them. Besides, he was only going to teach Humps to defend himself. "You want to spar?" Colin asked.

"Okay. I be Joe Louis, you be Billy Conn."

"Well, tie my gloves."

Humps tied the laces of Colin's gloves and called for one of his sisters to tie the gloves on his hands. Together they walked out to a hard packed strip of ground between the shack and the barn. "We're just going to spar," Colin said, trying to touch gloves with Humps who didn't understand touching gloves and thought Colin was trying to hit him with both hands. "We're supposed to touch gloves," Colin explained, but even then Humps reached out as though he were trying to feel with his hands.

Colin danced around on his toes, throwing light punches at Humps' shoulders and midsection while Humps blundered after him. Colin found sparring to be to his advantage. Being faster, he danced in, lightly cuffed Humps with both hands, and danced away before the heavier Humps could react. He was having fun.

Colin felt good as he danced around, bobbing and weaving the way he had seen them do in the films. He teased Humps by extending his chin, and when Humps swung at it, he countered with a quick jab to the nose. He toyed with Humps, stepping inside the roundhouse blows and tapping Humps with his gloves open. Humps was panting.

Frustrated by the elusive target, Humps charged after Colin, only to have Colin tie him up, spin him around, and dance away again. The more frustrated Humps became, the harder he tried to hit Colin, the easier a target he became. Colin laughed. "You ain't boxing, you clowning," Humps said.

"This is the way you are supposed to box," Colin said.

"No, it ain't. That ain't boxing, that's running around in circles."

"What do you want me to do?" Colin asked. He struck an exaggerated, hands extended palms up, John L. Sullivan pose and Humps hit him with a hard right to the nose that knocked him back a step and brought tears to his eyes. He ducked another punch and backed away, tasting blood in his mouth.

The punch had caught Colin by surprise but more surprising was the recognition that Humps was trying to hurt him. He couldn't understand it. He had only been teasing Humps. He wasn't trying to hurt him. When Humps swung another haymaker, Colin stepped inside and hit him with solid left, right punches. The cap slid across Humps' face and fell to the ground. Humps accidentally stepped on it. He stopped and looked at his new cap in dismay. "You made me ruin my new cap," he said.

Anger blazed in Humps' eyes and he began the attack again with renewed vigor. Colin backed away, circling, trying to stay out of Humps' range. He threw a punch at Humps' head that brought blood to his nose. Colin was surprised at the blood, at the look of pain on Humps' face. It wasn't supposed to hurt. Colin wanted to quit. He didn't mean to hurt Humps. He didn't want Humps to hurt him. He backed up and raised his open hands but Humps threw a punch that went between them and hit him in the face. Colin realized with a shock that Humps was trying to beat him. Actually trying to prove he was better. Not only that, Humps believed he could beat him.

Colin backed away, trying to protect his face with his hands, knowing he had little chance in a stand-up fight. Humps stalked him, grimly pressing, willing to take punches to get in one himself. Humps was getting in close and some of the punches were landing, stinging his ears and thumping his ribs.

Colin kept the jab in Humps' face, raising a welt over his

eye, but Humps kept after him. He hit Humps as hard as he could, the shock of the punch traveling up his arm and shoulder, rising to his head with joy. Hurting Humps felt good, and he tried to hurt him again although his ears rang, his ribs hurt, and his nose dripped blood. He hadn't started the fight and he wasn't going to run.

It was no longer enough to tease Humps, to toy with him, to defend himself. He wanted to humiliate Humps, to make Humps admit defeat. He stopped dancing and swung wildly, blindly, trying only to hurt, his own pain forgotten in the joy of hurting someone else. A blow spun him half around and once he fell to his knees but he kept swinging until he got to his feet again. He heard children's screams, a mother's calls, they meant nothing to him. He no longer had a goal, only a target.

Colin was stunned by the shock of cold water. He saw Willoliver standing with a bucket in his hand. Hump's sisters peered at him from behind their father's body. Humps' mother stood in the doorway, her fists clenched before her mouth. For a moment, Colin stood gasping. He saw Humps, also gasping, hands at his side.

"You fights like dogs, I treats you like dogs," Willoliver said. "Humps, get yourself in the house. Grown boy acting like an animal."

"I won, Papa," Humps said.

"You shut up, boy," Willoliver said, slapping Humps on the head. "You don't know nothing."

"You ruined your new shirt," Humps' mother wailed,

reaching out to him with one hand, the other still in her mouth.

Humps shirt was spotted with blood. Colin looked down at his own shirt. It too was blood-streaked.

Humps untied the laces with his teeth, smearing the white laces with blood. He dropped the gloves on the ground, picked up his cap, brushed it against his pants leg, gave Colin a long look, and walked undefeated into the nigrah shack.

Colin picked up the gloves. A fine layer of dust had stuck to the sweat and blood. He wiped them on his shirt, and walked to the windmill on shaky legs. His knees trembled and his arms ached. He washed the blood from his face and rinsed his mouth. He let the cold water run over his face. The water splashed on his new gloves, getting them wet, but he didn't care. He wished he hadn't gotten them. He wished it weren't Christmas. He turned off the tap and sat hunched over his knees. He didn't want to go to the house and there wasn't any place else to go.

After a while his father came to get him for Christmas dinner. His father looked at his face. "You been fighting with Humps?"

"Yeah."

"Well, you don't want to go to the house looking like that. Go in the back door and I'll get you a clean shirt. And wash your face good." His father examined him more closely. "What are you going to tell your mother and sister?"

"I won."

His father nodded. "If you fight a nigrah you have to beat him or he won't have any respect for you. Now, come on, Champ, your mother's got dinner ready."

Colin got up, already a little stiff. He did not feel victorious. He felt empty. He felt sad remembering the hurt and challenge in Humps' eyes. Colin didn't know if he had won or not. He knew if he had won, it wasn't any fun. He also knew it was not over.

TUMBLEWEED CHRISTMAS

Lucille stepped from the long, yellow school bus and walked slowly down the dirt road toward home. She pulled her too-short coat closer around her but she couldn't protect her thin, uncovered legs from the cold, biting, sand-filled wind that blew against them. It was the last day of school before Christmas.

She looked at the flat, brown land, empty of life for the winter and felt the same emptiness inside herself. Her father didn't want Christmas in the house. "You're too big for a tree," he said. He didn't want any of it, not the carols, or the wreaths, or even the joy. Not since Lucille's mother had died.

Although she was only twelve, Lucille understood that it was not because her mother had died, but because her father hadn't been able to give her anything while she was alive. The house wasn't their own. They had no car. Their clothes were worn and secondhand. But Lucille knew that her mother had been happy. Her mother had the liveliest eyes in town. Everyone said that. Eyes that sparkled like lights on a Christmas tree. Thinking about her mother's eyes made Lucille want to cry.

Lucille put her books and the gift-wrapped package she

had brought from school on the table. She didn't have time to cry. She had to clean the house, tend the animals, and fix supper.

Like her mother, Lucille didn't mind hard work. "Hands that can't find work can't find ease either," her mother used to say.

For a long time after he hurt his back working on Mr. Walser's barn, her father could not get a job. He went from house to house all day asking for any kind of work. Lucille took care of the animals, the house, and the garden, and her mother cleaned house and ironed for other people.

"I'm going to make it up to you," he kept saying to them both. "You'll see. Christmas is going to come." It seemed like he had been saying that for as long as she could remember. But it wasn't his fault. When he got a job at the meat packing house there was such a difference in the way he came home, in the way he said, "Christmas is going to come this year."

Then her mother got sick, and in spite of all the doctor could do, she died. It started all over again. Her father almost hopelessly in debt and no light in his eyes, not even a promise of Christmas this year.

"You're too big for birthdays," he said. Why couldn't he realize she would never be too big for Christmas trees and birthdays but she was big enough to understand he couldn't give her a present? Why couldn't he just say "Happy birthday" or "Merry Christmas" and smile at her again?

Just as she couldn't stop the West Texas wind from blowing, she couldn't stop the tears from falling. She hung her cup towel over the sink to dry and grabbed the bucket to go milk. She angrily brushed the tears aside.

The tears went away but the anger did not, and when Old Brown kicked at the milk bucket, Lucille hit the cow in the flank. When the chickens got so excited they turned over their pan and spilled all the feed, she lashed out at them, too.

"Why does he have to be so mean to himself?" she asked the pigs. "There'll be no Thanksgiving in this house," she mimicked her father. She had known there wouldn't be turkey. She didn't even like turkey. She knew he wouldn't kill a hen, he'd sold all the culls. She just wanted them to eat together, but he had volunteered to work that day because they needed the money. He had come in too tired to eat. Lucille had eaten alone. She was glad when Thanksgiving was over and she could go back to school.

Lucille liked school. She liked reading about other places, and learning new things. Reading poetry was her favorite because it made her insides sparkle like Mama's eyes had. But the first time she had looked into a microscope was almost as exciting. And learning about Thomas Jefferson and Joan of Arc. She wished she could stay in school forever, even if some of the children made fun of her clothes.

"You should never be embarrassed about your clothes as long as they are mended, clean, and ironed," Mama used to say. She hadn't been except for the time Papa had seen her in one of Mama's dresses. She wasn't embarrassed exactly, but it felt like being embarrassed.

It was a special day in the school, the day for school pictures, and she wanted a special dress. She had opened her mother's closet and there her things were, as though she were still alive. She had chosen the blue polka dot dress with the velvet ribbon. She had thought Papa wouldn't mind, and he hadn't exactly. He mistook her for her mother. "Rosa," he said, and his voice conveyed his shock of happiness, but his face betrayed the disappointment that it was Lucille in Rosa's dress.

"I'm sorrry, Papa," she said, but he couldn't look at her, not when she was wearing her mother's dress, and he seemed unable to speak to her about her mother. Later he would not allow her to help as he neatly packed her mother's things to take to the church for the needy. "There are those who need them more than you," he said and she nodded. She knew that he did not want to be reminded of Rosa everytime he saw her dresses. But she wished he would talk to her about Mama.

Lucille set the heavy bucket of milk on the table and looked at the package that was already covered with a fine coat of dust. What was she going to do with her Christmas present for Papa? All the children made Christmas presents for their parents at school. She wished she had explained to her teacher why she couldn't give Papa a gift. She was afraid of being embarrassed in front of her class by telling the teacher her father couldn't afford a present for her and her gift to him would make him unhappy.

Besides, it wasn't just a present for Papa, it was a present to her from the teacher. The teacher gave the children a school picture of themselves, and the end of an orange crate to decorate as the picture frame. She brought scraps of paper, cloth, and paint to the school. Lucille had made a background out of the soft, cushiony paper from a candy box.

Some of the boys heated metal rods and burned designs into the rough wooden crate frame. Some of the girls brought satin or flannel from home and glued it to the frame. Lucille decided to paint hers. There were only two kinds of paint—cow barn red and locomotive black. The Murphy twins wanted the red and Lucille knew better than to argue with them. She painted hers black. She cut out of old magazines pictures of the things she loved—horses, dogs, elephants, rabbits, and bluebonnets. The other children laughed but her teacher said it was original and gave her a gold star to glue to the top of the frame.

Lucille liked the picture of herself in Mama's dress, surrounded by the things she loved with a bright gold star over her head. But she remembered the look on Papa's face and hid the package under clothes in a drawer. She would decide later what to do with it.

On Christmas Eve, Lucille went about her chores singing carols all day. Maybe Papa would walk to town with her like they used to with Mama to see the lights and decorations, and hear the music, and look in the windows, and watch the children in their excitement and expectations.

Papa was finishing the meal she had prepared before going to milk when Lucille returned to the house. "Lucille, I'm going to have to go back to work tonight and will work a shift tomorrow. It means you will be home alone on Christmas Day, but we need the money."

Lucille busied herself putting away the milk so Papa would not know how disappointed she was. "Yes, Papa," she said.

"I'm going to go now."

"Can I go, Papa?" she asked without thinking.

"No," Papa said. "I'm going straight to work. I won't be coming home."

"Please, Papa," she said. "I can walk home by myself." The plea escaped from her. He thought she would be disappointed seeing all the things she couldn't have, but she wouldn't be. She just wanted to be a part of Christmas for a little while.

"I don't have time," he said.

She didn't cry until after he was gone.

There were no tears Christmas Day when she began her chores. She was a big girl, almost a woman, and what did Christmas mean but thinking of others beside herself.

She knew what she would do. She would have a Christmas party for the animals and give herself the picture she had made at school. She would fix little presents for Old Brown, and for the hens, and the chickens, and the pigs. She would invite them all to the barn, and sing carols to them, and give them their presents.

She wished she had a Christmas tree. Any kind of tree would do. Even the limb off a tree would do. But they had no trees except the pecan tree and she dared not break a limb off the pecan tree. Papa picked up the pecans and sold them, but he would never thrash the limbs, or allow her to climb into the tree and shake its branches.

"The pecan tree is good to us," Papa said. "What kind of people would we be if we hurt it taking its presents?"

She had given up on the tree when she noticed the tumbleweeds that had blown up against the garden fence.

A tumbleweed Christmas tree.

All morning Lucille worked building and decorating the tumbleweed Christmas tree. She almost burst with excitement choosing just the right tumbleweeds and carrying them one by one to the barn where she had cleared a place for her party. She put three tumbleweeds together for the base, then two and then one small one for the top, until it was the biggest tree she had ever seen.

She cut the star off the chicken feed sack and stuck it on top. Old Brown's rope was not the color she preferred but she wrapped it around the tree several times. She found some plastic rings that Papa had used when he culled the hens and hung them on the stems of the tumbleweeds. Then she shelled some corn and cut the corn cobs in round slices and hung them for balls.

Lucille ran to the house, for once not minding the cold wind that chapped her face and stung her legs. She had forgotten all discomforts in her excitement about her Christmas party. She took a box from the closet shelf where Mama had saved used wrapping paper and bows and carefully chose three pieces of paper with bows to match.

Back in the barn she wrapped her little presents of shelled corn for the pigs, bread crumbs for the chickens, and a cottonseed cake for Old Brown.

Lucille placed the presents for the animals along with

her own under the tumbleweed Christmas tree, then brought the animals to the small shed that Papa called the barn, and sang carols to them. Old Brown listened while patiently chewing her cud, the chickens eyed the presents with curiosity, but Lucille had to scold the pigs that were interested in nothing but what was under the tree.

Lucille was having so much fun she didn't know when Papa entered the barn. She might not have noticed him at all except that Old Brown stopped chewing her cud and the chickens turned their curiosity from the presents to the barn door. The pigs did not seem to notice Papa at all, and when Lucille saw him and stopped singing, they rushed in, tore the packages, and ate some of Old Brown's cottonseed cake before Lucille noticed and chased them away.

"Mean old pigs," she said, close to tears.

Papa sat down beside her and put his arms around her. The pigs kept their distance, looking over their shoulders. They were afraid of Papa.

"I was going to give the animals their presents and the pigs ruined it all," she said.

Papa tidied up the packages, smoothing out the torn paper and rewrapping the cottonseed cake.

"There," he said, "Whose present is this?"

"Old Brown's," Lucille said.

Papa opened the torn package and gave the cake to Old Brown. "And whose present is this?"

"The pigs'," Lucille said.

"Let's make them wait until last," Papa said, taking the other package and spreading the bread crumbs for the chickens. Only then did he notice that there was an extra present and looked at Lucille. She couldn't speak. "I'll bet this is for me," he said. He gave the corn to the noisy pigs before opening his gift.

"It's a beautiful frame, and a beautiful picture of a beautiful girl and I'm going to keep them forever," he said. He hugged her and kissed the top of her head.

Then he reached into his pocket and pulled out a little package wrapped in silver with red ribbon and a red bow. "Whose present is this?" he asked. It was the prettiest thing Lucille had ever seen, but she could not speak. "It must be for you," Papa said, placing it in her hand.

"Oh, Papa, thank you, it is so pretty," she said, thinking how much such paper and ribbon must cost. She held it to her cheek.

"Aren't you going to open it?" Papa asked.

Lucille couldn't believe it. There was another present inside. "I don't want to tear it," she said, a tear trickling down her face. The package was too perfect to spoil.

Papa slipped the bow from the package and put it in her hair. He took off the ribbon and tied it around her wrist. He unwrapped the paper and smoothed it and placed it on the ground beside her. He handed her a blue velvet box that was the prettiest thing she had ever seen.

She took the box in her hand, feeling the soft fur of the velvet, and held it to her cheek. "Open it," Papa said. Lucille couldn't believe it. Inside the box was another present. Slowly she opened the box, and inside the box on a bed of satin lay a beautiful gold watch with a leather band.

It was the most beautiful watch she had ever seen, so beautiful it frightened her. It was not a watch like any of the other children had. It was not a watch for a little girl. Lucille was confused. She could only stare at it. Papa took the watch and placed it on her wrist. Then he hugged her tight.

"I was going to give it to your mother," he said. "I put it in layaway last Christmas because I wanted her to have something fine. I worked overtime to pay for it so I wouldn't take anything away from you. When she was sick, I asked the jeweler to let me take it for a little while so she could see it, so she would know that this year Christmas was going to come. She said that you and me, we were the only Christmas she ever needed."

Papa stopped and Lucille thought he was going to cry; instead he scolded the pigs that were trying to get the last of the chickens' bread crumbs. Then he continued, "When your mother died, I knew that her watch must belong to you. That's why there was no birthday and no Thanksgiving. I was able to get it last night only because the plant paid me for the work I would do today."

"Papa, it is a watch for a woman."

"It is a watch for my daughter because she has worked like a woman. Wear it with pride."

"Oh, I will never wear it, Papa. I will keep it in the little box where I can look at it from time to time and think of Mama."

"No, Lucille, a watch is to wear. A watch is for the present, not the past."

"But Papa, I couldn't bear it if I lost Mama's watch."

"It is your watch, Lucille. You must take care of it, but if you lose it, you still have this moment. Christmas is not the watch, Lucille. Christmas will last long after the watch is gone."

"Oh, Papa," Lucille said. Her Papa was the smartest man in the whole world.

"You are the only Christmas I'll ever need," Papa said. "I will try to keep your picture and frame forever, but if I can't, I will still have this moment."

"Oh, Papa," Lucille said, giving him a kiss. She looked just in time to see one of the pigs take the beautiful silver wrapping paper in its mouth. One of the other pigs tried to take it away, tearing it. But Lucille did not cry. She remembered what it was like when it was perfect.

PLACE

Louise had always known this day would come. Her father would come back. That was the way it had always been. Whenever she and her brother, Tom, had forgotten him and begun making a life of their own, he always came back; sick, destitute, defeated. She and Tom always had to postpone their plans for a while in order to take care of him. As soon as he had recovered enough to help out, he left them with their broken plans and new debts. But they could never leave him. Louise knew she could never go far enough to be free of him.

She had ignored the letters from Tom and his wife, Dorothy, because she did not want to think about her father or going home. That was another life and she wanted to be free of it. She had her own life now. It was a clean life, filled with rewards, plans, the satisfaction of bills paid, a little money saved, and the slow, systematic accumulation of the materials to make a home.

But she could ignore the signs no longer. Last night when Tom called, he had been excited. He had exaggerated their father's condition. He had made wild threats about what he was going to do and gloomy predictions about what was going to happen—signs she knew only too well. Years earlier, when Tom was in the sixth grade and Louise in the fifth, their father had written a hot check at the grocery store. Louise and Tom had to drop out of school for a while and pick cotton to pay back the money and get their father out of jail. When the school bus passed by, they lay down in the field hoping the other children wouldn't see them.

"What kind of birds are there?" their classmates called on those wet days when they couldn't pick cotton and had to return to school.

"Redbirds, bluebirds, and jailbirds," the others responded.

Tom was going to kill their tormentors, he was going to set their houses on fire. He predicted that their father would never get out of jail, that they would starve to death, that the state would take them away and put them in foster homes. Louise went to school when she could and when she couldn't she tried to keep up with her homework so she would not drop behind her classmates. Tom got behind, failed a grade, avoided school when he could, and dropped out as soon as he was old enough.

When their father couldn't get a job, and had left owing money to half the people in town, Tom had threatened to go find his father. He was going to beat him up, he was going to make him pay the money back. He predicted they would spend the rest of their lives paying off their father's debts. Louise had gone to the grocery store to ask for more credit. Tom had lied about his age and joined the Navy.

When their father came back, Tom was in the Navy and Louise was in Wichita Falls, working and going to college.

He found her, of course, and she had taken him in, sobered him, and for a while it had worked. He washed dishes at the cafe where she was a waitress. They were almost a family, until he started drinking again. He lost his job. He took money from her purse. When she confronted him with it, he lied, then he cried and promised it would never happen again. She told him he had to stay sober and get a job. And she kept her money with her at all times. While she was at work he sold her school books and left. The next time he came back, she and Tom put him in a nursing home with Louise paying the bill.

Now he was back, living with Tom and his wife and two children, and Tom was getting ready to run, too. She knew the signs too well. She had to go back to that place where she would always be who she had been, poor little jailbird's daughter; back to that time when she was both orphan and mother.

Although Tom was older, he had too much pride to ask for help. It had been up to her to plead for credit, for any kind of work. Now it was up to her to save Tom from their father. As soon as she could make arrangements for someone to take her senior English classes.

Tom had hated school. He didn't like someone else telling him what to do and pointing out his mistakes. Tom didn't understand why she had always gone back to school no matter how often she had to drop out or how much fun the other children made of her, why she had become a teacher, why she was still going to school.

It was true there was little money in teaching and less

prestige. Women assumed she was a teacher because she couldn't find a husband, men assumed she was a teacher because she couldn't do anything else. But it was in school that she discovered there was a life of the mind, the spirit, something beyond the end of the cotton row. School had liberated her and she wanted to free others to discover the poetry she believed was in all of them. Maybe she'd never own a home, always drive a secondhand car, spend summers going to school, but it was her life and when one muted child said, "Miss Patterson, would you look at what I've written; I think it's a poem," it was worth all those years of picking cotton, begging for credit, working and going to school, applying for scholarships, being scorned by sororities and those who passed out honors for social acceptability.

She couldn't understand why, after the Navy, Tom had gone back to that place they both vowed to escape. Where he had to drive thirty miles every day to work in the tire company in Center Point. Where he had to live next door to people who had called, "redbirds, bluebirds, and jailbirds." Or why he had married the youngest of the three Dismuke girls. The older two had dropped out of school because they were pregnant. Dottie had fallen in love with Tom in his sailor suit and dropped out of school to marry him. Louise couldn't understand why Tom had promptly fathered two children he could ill-afford and who would tie him to the mindless, menial work he had despised his father for doing.

Louise didn't want to go back to that. She didn't want to see her father, not in the condition he had gotten himself in. She didn't like her father. No, it was more than that. She didn't love her father.

Nevertheless, she talked to her principal, arranged for a substitute, and outlined what her classes should do until she returned. It was a four-hour drive from Fort Worth to Wanderer Springs and she spent the time reviewing her dreams, checking her willingness to surrender them. She wanted to complete her Master's Degree and then attempt the Ph.D. It wasn't because she wanted to go into administration, or because she wanted to teach in college; she wanted to be the best she could be. She had already gone far beyond what anyone had believed her capable of, and the Ph.D. represented the ultimate in her profession.

Sometimes, burdened with rent, car payments, night classes, and papers to grade, she had dreamed of a life of ease, of being taken care of by a man, but she knew that wasn't what she wanted. What she wanted was a husband to work alongside her towards goals they both shared. She wanted someone to give dimension to the quiet times, stability to the good times, cheer to the times when everything went wrong.

She wanted children, not just as objects of mutual worship, but because she had learned so much about life and she wanted to teach it outside the strictures of school to someone who was uniquely hers. Because she had to work and go to school, it had taken her longer than most teachers to be certified. Already she was twenty-eight, halfway to a master's degree, and no prospective husband and father in sight. There were no eligible men at her school, she spent most evenings working on her night classes and most weekends grading papers. And she was approaching another responsibility as fast as traffic laws allowed.

It was late when she arrived at her brother's house, a small, unpainted, four-room house on a dirt street. The front door was open and through the screen door she could hear the television and see Tom and Dorothy waiting up for her, sitting together on a broken-springed couch. "Come on in, Lou," Tom called. With a tired little smile, Dorothy got up to let her in. Dorothy was still pretty, but she had married too young, and her tall figure had been misshapen by children.

"I brought a couple of books for the children," Louise said.

"Oh thanks," Dorothy said without enthusiasm. Louise had given books to the children since they were born. She had never seen Tom or Dorothy read to them, or the children pick up the books by themselves, but she had not given up hope. "The kids are asleep but you can wake them up if you want to," Dorothy said.

"I'll see them in the morning," Louise said. She walked into the living room. Her father was sitting in a faded, lumpy stuffed chair. He did not look up when she came into the room.

"I think he's learned his lesson this time, Louise," Tom said. Their father seemed to be unaware that he was the subject of the conversation. "He's gotten as low as he can get." Tom rested his long thin face in his cupped hand. He drummed his long, knotted, grease-stained fingers against his cheek, and squinted his eyes in sincerity. The more uncertain Tom was, the more definite he became.

"I told Tom I can't stand this," Dorothy said. "I can't leave him for a minute, and I can't invite anyone in with him here." Dot's two sisters lived nearby, one without a husband, the other with a husband who was not the father of her children. The three sisters got together to drink coffee and gossip while the children played. "You're going to have to do something."

"Dad, how are you?" Louise asked, patting her father's hand. The hand was crusty and lifeless. He recognized her when she spoke. He did not seem surprised to see her. He didn't even seem curious.

Tom and Dorothy watched without interest. Tom lighted a cigarette and inhaled so deeply he etched lines in his cheeks.

"I'm not feeling too well," her father said, his eyes on the television screen, his voice high-pitched and breathless. His jaw was slack and his breath came irregularly through his mouth. His face was drawn and his eyes seemed big and staring. He had always been small, but Louise was shocked at how he had wasted away; how dry his skin was; how gray his hair had become.

"You should have seen him when Tom brought him home," Dorothy said. "You could practically see through him." She no longer had time to take care of her long, blonde hair, or her nails, and her hands and small oval face were beginning to roughen.

"What's the matter, Dad?"

"I can't seem to get my strength back. I just can't seem

to do nothing. I've really done it this time," he said. "I don't ever want to be in this shape again."

Louise was not convinced. She had heard it before.

"How are you getting along?" he asked without interest, without looking at her, taking a short breath and running a stiff hand over his dead, gray hair. "Everything all right down your way?"

"Just fine." No one in the room wanted to hear about her paper on Ezra Pound, her senior honors class, or Tien Thai who knew no English and had just been added to her class.

"Found a husband yet?"

"No." She tried to hide her anger. That was the only question he ever asked, as though her lack of a husband were the only remaining connection between them.

Her father turned his attention to the television screen, making himself small, trying to slip away from them, to disappear before their eyes. Louise looked at her brother.

"Like I told you," he said. "The police called and told me he was spending nights in the Wichita Falls bus station and that if I didn't come get him they were going to put him in jail for loitering. I don't know where he came from."

"Dad," Louise said, touching his knee to get his attention. "Where have you been?"

"Around. Mostly out west."

Louise knew what that meant. Hitchhiking from place to place, panhandling for food or drink, sleeping in doorways and under bridges; one of that tattered army that marched under the white flag. Sometimes Louise saw them in Fort

Worth, lonely, wretched men in urine-stained trousers, waiting for a handout, a liquor store to open, a meal at the Salvation Army. She looked at them sharply, thinking she might find her father, then hurried away.

"Why did you come back?" she asked.

"I haven't been feeling too well. I can't get a job, I can't do nothing."

"What do you plan to do?"

"I don't guess there's anything I can do," he said, setting his jaw.

Louise looked at Tom. He shrugged his shoulders. "Pop, we have to decide something while Louise is here," Tom said.

"What would you like to do?" Louise persisted.

"I don't guess I can do what I'd like to do," he said, trying to laugh. A string of saliva ran out one corner of his mouth and he wiped it away with the back of his hand. "I'd like to start all over. Get me a good job. Be a father to you kids."

"It's too late for that," Tom said.

He nodded, not looking at either of them. "I did the best I could," he said.

"You can't stay here," Louise said.

"No, I don't have no place here."

"Where do you plan to go?"

"I don't guess there is any place I can go," he said with a touch of the old anger and impatience. Trembling, he began to cry.

Louise ignored the tears. "Dad, you're still a young man," Louise said. "You're, what, fifty-five? That's not old. You have a lot of life ahead of you. You have to make plans how you want to spend it."

"I didn't plan to end up like this," he said. "I didn't plan to come back here and be a burden on you kids."

"You didn't plan anything," Tom said. "As long as I can remember, you didn't plan anything. You didn't plan for Mother to die so you didn't take her to the hospital. You didn't plan to go to jail so you wrote a hot check. You didn't plan to pay off your debts so you ran away and left them for me and Lou to pay."

"Okay, Tom, there's no need to go into that," Louise said. "We can't do anything about the past, let's see if we can do something about the future." Dorothy chewed at a fingernail. Tom shifted his weight on the couch. "Are you just going to sit around for the rest of your life?" Louise asked her father.

"No."

"What are you going to do?"

The old crafty look came in his eye. "Soon as I get my strength back I'm going to California," he said. "I'll need some money."

"Where are you going to get it?"

"I thought maybe you or Tom would loan it to me. I ain't no good to you here."

"Louise, could you do something? I'm barely making enough to feed my two kids," Tom said. He looked anxiously at his hands as though expecting them to fail him.

It was tempting but temporary. In a few weeks or months their father would be back in worse condition than now. "There are four adults in this room," Louise said. "We have to decide what is best for everyone. And loaning you a few dollars is not it, Dad."

"I think we should give him the money if we have it," Tom said. "Let him go with the understanding that he's never coming back. If you come back here I'll let them put you in jail, Dad. Don't you come back here."

Their father began to cry again and Louise put a hand around his shoulder and patted his arm. The flesh was flaccid and unresisting and her hand went almost around his upper arm. For a moment, Louise thought she was going to be sick. She looked at Tom. "He wouldn't last a week on his own," she said.

"I just can't stand it any more," Dorothy said. She wiped her eyes with a corner of her dress. "Maybe we should put him some place—some kind of institution," she said.

Louise remembered the time they had put him in the nursing home. He had stayed for two weeks, until he felt better, then he left. They did not hear from him until the police called from Wichita Falls. "What kind of institution?" she asked without hope.

"I think he's crazy," Tom said, blowing ashes off the end of his cigarette. "He doesn't recognize me half the time."

"He just sits there," Dorothy said.

"Can't you see the way he looks?" Tom asked. "We can have him put in the state hospital."

"He can't remember anything," Dorothy said. "He asks the same questions all day long."

Her father was slumped in his chair, his jaw slack, staring vacantly at the television. Louise was tempted. Her father was not insane but for a moment she almost wished he were. Just to have it done with, to never have to worry again about where he was, how he was, whether he was alive. "No," Louise said. She did not believe her father was crazy. If they could get him in an institution where he would be helped—but she feared he would be put in an alcoholic ward and forgotten. For the rest of his life. Fifteen or twenty years. "No."

"Then what do you plan to do with him?" Tom asked.

"Dad," Louise said, waiting for his attention to focus on her. "Dad, if you don't take control of your life, you're going to end up in a state hospital. What do you want to do?"

"It don't seem right that a man should work all his life and not have no place to go," he said, beginning to cry again.

"If he had ever done anything for us it would be different," Tom said. "But as long as I can remember, we've had to give up whatever we wanted to take care of him."

"As long as he has you all to look after him, he's not going to do one thing for himself," Dorothy said.

Louise looked at her father. He was trying to disappear again, to become so small they forgot he was there. He had given up. Then why not let him go? Put him in the state hospital. Write a weekly letter. Visit him at Thanksgiving and Christmas. It was so appealing.

"I've already talked to a doctor in Center Point," Tom said. "He said he'd sign the papers but we have to have two doctors sign it. I thought you might want to talk to one."

"Okay," Louise said. "I'll talk to the doctor."

"You'd better go to Hill. I don't think Dr. Posey will sign it."

"How many doctors did you talk to?"

"Two. Dr. Posey won't sign it."

Then it wasn't a matter of getting a doctor to sign the papers, it was going from doctor to doctor until she found one who would sign the papers. "I could take him home with me," she offered without conviction.

Dorothy looked quickly at Tom. Louise knew that had been their plan. The state hospital was for them also the last resort. "Are you sure you want to?" Dorothy asked.

"What will you do with him while you're at school?" Tom asked.

It was hopeless. She didn't believe in her father any more. She wondered when she stopped believing in her family, that they could support and sustain each other. She wondered if she believed in anything. She still believed in education, that education could liberate Tien Thai to a useful and meaningful life. But not her father. He was too old. Not Tom or Dorothy either. When had that happened, she wondered? When had she given up?

Her teachers hadn't given up on her. Miss Duckworth hadn't. Old Duckwalk they had called her when they were kind. No one liked her because she was old, and grim, and walked like a duck. Once Louise had missed two weeks of school and the day she returned, they had a test. It was Algebra and she hadn't understood one question. She had gone home in tears, ready to quit school like Tom. That night old Duckwalk had come to the house and while Louise ironed shirts to pay the grocery bill, Miss Duckworth explained Algebra.

"I can't do it," Louise had cried. "I just can't."

"I'm not going to do it for you," Miss Duckworth had said, as grim as ever. "But I'll make it possible for you to do it."

And she had done it, but Louise had been willing to try. Old Duckwalk didn't give her anything, not even half a point on a test grade. She had done it herself. She hadn't just quit. Why couldn't her father at least try? She knew it had been hard for him when her mother died, when they were hungry and there was no food in the house, when he couldn't get any kind of job and he owed everyone. They could have worked it out. But he had deserted them. He had run away when they needed him. And now, when he needed them, he came back and expected them to work out his problems. And they couldn't desert him. They would never be free of him the way he had been free of. . . .

But he hadn't passed them off on other relatives. He hadn't turned them over to the state or an orphanage. He never completely went away. He always came back.

"Dad," she said, taking his hand in both of hers. "Why did you hang around Wichita Falls? You could have come here. You could have kept moving, but you hung around Wichita Falls until you became a nuisance. Why?"

"I wasn't feeling well. I was tired."

"But why this place?"

"I just wanted to be close," he said, so softly she hardly heard.

"Then why didn't you come here? Why didn't you come to Tom on your own?"

Instead of answering, he hung his head, and began to cry, blubbering now. He couldn't, or wouldn't, speak but she thought she understood. He was torn between love and shame. He loved them too much to entirely leave them, but he was too ashamed of himself to ask them to take him in. He had wasted his life and made theirs more difficult, but there was still a spark of father's love.

"It's all right, Dad. This is where you should have come. We're your family."

"He knew if he came back here we'd have to take him in," Tom said.

"Dad, listen. You can come home with me. But you will have to be responsible for yourself. You will have to make your own decisions. I will not give up my dreams. I will not be your mother. I will not live your life for you, but you can come home with me."

"I want to go back to California," he said.

"Then go. It's your decision, but we're not going to help you." She looked at Tom, daring him to offer help. "If you want to go to California, then you get up and get yourself there."

"I can't do nothing. I don't feel well," he said, his chin trembling.

She realized he was scared. He had never believed in

himself and it was a long time since anyone else had. "You don't have to be responsible for us any more, Dad. You were a good teacher. You taught us to take care of ourselves. And now we're going to help you, but we're not going to let you run over us. Now, do you want to go home with me, or do you want to hit the road to California?"

"I don't have any money."

"You got here without any money."

He was angry, but that was okay, as long as he wasn't apathetic. "I can't do nothing."

"We'll start slow, but you have to go to Alcoholics Anonymous, you have to get a job and you have to do your share of the work. You are not a guest."

"What if I can't get a job?"

"You'll keep trying until you do."

"What if I can't stay sober?"

She looked at him and saw her own doubt reflected in his face. She knew that Tom and Dorothy didn't believe in him either. Why didn't she just give up? Why didn't she just let him go? "We can't do it for you, Dad. All we can do is make it possible for you to do it. All we can do is try."

He took a deep but shaky breath. "Dot, if I'm going with Lou I guess you better pack my bag," he said.

"Pack it yourself," Louise said.

Dorothy and Tom both looked at her, afraid he would quit, that he would slide away from them once more. Louise could tell he was thinking about it. He got up and shuffled out of the room. "I hope he doesn't pack everything we have and sell it for liquor," Dot said.

"We have to start some place," Louise said.

"Do you think it'll work?" Dorothy asked.

"I don't know. I know I have to try. Tom, I know you're scared. So am I. So is he. But we haven't been a family since Mother died. This is our chance."

"If he gets to drinking you can send him back here for a while," Dorothy said. "I can watch after him for a while."

Tom lighted a cigarette, inhaling so deeply he etched lines in his cheeks. "What can I do?" he asked.

Louise smiled. She didn't know how he could help, but he was willing to learn.

Their father came back in the room with his things in a grocery bag and sat down. He looked at her. "Lou, I ain't good for much," he said.

"I'll bet you could get a job washing dishes," she said.

"I bet I could," he said. Some happy memory brought a faint glimmer of light to his eyes. "I reckon until I do I could practice on yours," he said. He almost smiled.

THE BOY FROM CHILLICOTHE

Randy Sims walked along the quiet, darkening street nodding to the few people he saw. It was late spring, and along about dark, after the family had eaten and the teenagers had escaped in the family car, the older folks and the younger ones would sit on the front porch and drink iced tea or lemonade, or stand out in the yard in undershirts and cotton dresses talking quietly to the folks next door in muffled voices and ripples of laughter that dissipated pleasantly in the street. It was the time of fireflies and glowing cigarettes, and the tinkle of ice in heavy glasses; the time of lurid, flickering shadows and clipped, incisive voices and brittle laughter that split the silence and ricocheted down the street, the time of three horsepower lawnmowers and glass pack mufflers that tear the air like an old wound.

Randy walked along the path that ran like a scar across the grass lawns. His step was slow and deliberate. He liked walking alone in the darkness. "Hello, Randy," folks would say. "How's the boy from Chillicothe?" They did not have to be in awe of anyone from Chillicothe.

The people of Wanderer Springs, being for the most part farmers and shirt-sleeved merchants, had little education themselves, but they had an enormous respect for it in others. For this reason, the teachers in the town enjoyed a special caste, and few could come boldly into their presence. But Randy was different. He was from Chillicothe, an almost identical small town down the road. They thought him like themselves: careless of the world, independent of progress, immune to dreams, interested in chicken diseases, the efficacy of fertilizer, and the virtues of contour rows.

Randy crossed the street and went around the big gray house with the gable and stained glass window, to the little cottage in back. The cottage had formerly been a double garage, but when the husband had died, the widow had sold the two cars, converted the garage into a cottage, and retired to the house for the rest of her life. The cottage was usually rented to some spinster teacher who expected to be soon married. There was a large living room with good furniture, a small, crowded kitchen with little light, no ventilation, and an unreliable oven, a small cluttered bedroom, and a dark, dingy bathroom. The living room was nice for entertaining but the rest of the house was not suited to resigned living. Those who lived in the cottage either married quickly or moved on to a more comfortable place.

Randy had been coming here two or three times a week for several months, and still he felt vaguely annoyed. It was as though he wished he were somewhere else, but could not make up his mind to go. He knocked irritably at the door.

"Is that you, Randy? Come on in." The cheerful voice fell unpleasantly on his ears.

Randy went in, looked around, and sat down on the couch. In the next room he could hear Hazel finishing her preparations, powdering her face, spraying her hair, uncapping her lipstick in a welter of contrasting odors, all of them sweet, feminine, and sticky. He knew with some regret that his annoyance would soon be gone and he would begin to enjoy himself.

Hazel Hickman was the new typing teacher, and the only teacher Randy's age. Because young people either married or left Wanderer Springs as soon as possible, and because the teachers were forbidden to date the students, Hazel and Randy were often together. At first, because they were both new, they had stayed close together at the teachers' meetings. Later, the brutal loneliness, the sense of nothing to do, the ache of necessity, drove them together until they were meeting two or three times a week in Hazel's apartment. In the way of small towns, people began predicting their marriage until every meeting was an unofficial announcement.

"How's the boy from Chillicothe? Starved?" Hazel asked, fastening her belt as she came into the room. She was wearing a black dress she could not wear at school. "Dinner's ready," she said, and glancing at him for the first time, she took his hand and led him into the small, hot kitchen.

Hazel was a big girl with thick short yellow hair. Her hands and feet were blunt, and her face broad but handsome. She had big placid eyes that were capable of blinking away any excitement. Randy was always disturbed by the eyes. He wanted to make them snap, or flash, or dilate, or anything except that slow wide-eyed blink. Despite her large frame, Hazel was shapely with a trim waist and firm hips. She moved with the slow and heavy grace of a young cow.

Hazel was from Dallas and hated the hard, meagre life of the small town. She did not like teaching school. She had prepared herself to teach, and had studied shorthand and typing as a safeguard against finishing college without getting married. She had hoped to teach or get an office job in some large town full of brilliant, eligible men, but her grades had been commonplace, her recommendations hesitant, and her shorthand inadequate. She had accepted the job in Wanderer Springs because she could do no better, and in Wanderer Springs there was no one but Randy.

At first, she had not been attracted to Randy. He was not as large a man as she had wanted; he was rather quiet and shy, and he was sensitive rather than rugged. But he was nice, intelligent, and he could get a job anywhere.

Hazel set the steaming dishes on the table, and uncovered them with pride. Hazel was not a good cook. She fixed light, exotic dishes which she prepared according to recipe with little imagination and frequent failure. Randy, used to the dreary, simple fare of the country, tasted the dishes with caution, ate little, and never felt satisfied. They ate quietly; Randy steeling his taste buds against shock, Hazel devoting herself entirely to eating.

"Go in the living room and look at a magazine, and I'll just stack the dishes," she said when they had finished.

"Shall I put on a record?"

"No. I thought tonight we'd just talk."

Randy was disappointed. He liked to dance with her.

Hazel was a good dancer, and he felt with pleasure her strong body moving in time with his own. Usually they would dance for a while, then sit on the couch and kiss until it was time for Randy to go. It was a comfort to him, and he was careful not to endanger their relationship. Randy was sure the evening would be a long one. They had never talked much, and then only about school. Hazel was not a good conversationalist.

Randy sat down on the couch, leaned back his head and closed his eyes. He thought of the cool darkness outside, and the pleasant space, and the stabbing loneliness. He was glad he had come.

When he felt her near him, he opened his eyes and took her hand, still damp with hand lotion, pulling her down on the couch beside him. He tried to kiss her but she turned away. He leaned back comfortably on the couch.

Hazel sat stiffly on the couch, twisting the college ring she wore on her left hand. "Randy, there's something I have to tell you," she said. "After I tell you, you may feel differently about me, but I have to be honest," she said deliberately, inspecting her nails.

Randy became instantly alert. She was adding something new to their relationship. Things were changing and he didn't like it. He shifted his weight on the couch. "You don't have to tell me anything," he said.

"But I do. We can't go on like this without your knowing."

Randy did not like the injection of responsibility into their relationship. In spite of their friendship, he still considered his problems his own. He wanted the freedom to come and go without the necessity of being involved in her blemishes and emotional pores. "I have no right to know," he protested.

But evidently Hazel thought he did, for she brushed aside every objection and insisted on telling her story.

In her last year of college, Hazel had become despondent. Soon she would be graduating and she had no prospect of getting married. Most girls her own age had already married. And if she graduated without getting married, where would she find an eligible man? He did not know how serious these things are to a girl. She slept fitfully at night, had to take long walks and hot baths to relax, and did badly in her classes.

There was one boy in school who seemed to think a lot of her. He was a large, rugged boy, a good dresser, who had come to school to play football, but had been unable to play because of his grades. She had dated him several times and she was sure he liked her, but he usually went with easy girls.

One of her girl friends, a psychology major, told her he was looking for his mother in all the girls, and if he ever once found her, he would be satisfied. She had never done anything wrong in her life, but her friend kept insisting that this was her chance, and the friend planted an idea in her mind that had never been there before.

Randy was appalled. She was justifying herself in the baldest way, and confessing a sexual error that is admitted, if at all, only on the presumption of a permanent relationship.

"I don't think you had better tell me any more," he said, standing up preparing to take his leave as quietly and painlessly as possible. "I enjoyed the dinner very much," he said.

But Hazel did not notice. She leaned forward and crossed her arms under her breasts. Her voice became excited.

"One night he said, 'I think you're the one for me. If only I could be sure.' And I said, 'I am the one.' "

She looked up at him, wringing her hands in her lap. Her lips were twisted and her brow furrowed in self-pity. The eyes were dull and painless. "I didn't know anything about men then," she cried. "He just grabbed me and had relations with me in the car."

Randy could feel himself being sucked in, but he could not help it. He sank down slowly on the couch. "You mean he . . . ?"

"I didn't want to. I told him I didn't."

"Did you tell anybody? Report it?"

"A girl can't tell a thing like that," she said, shaking her head at him in astonishment.

"But if he really . . . ?"

"I knew you wouldn't understand," she said. The large eyelids slowly closed and tears dampened her darkened lashes, smudging her cheek.

"I do understand," he said crossly, crossing his legs and hardening his heart. He did not intend to become involved.

"It's just that it's so . . . so terrible," he explained.

"I didn't enjoy it, if that's what you think," she said, looking at him frankly through clear eyes.

Randy sat up, and after straightening the creases in his trousers, he scratched his knee, stalling for time. "Let's not talk about it anymore," he said, slapping his knees and preparing to rise.

"But it isn't important," she said. "Don't you see? The important thing is that I didn't want to."

He offered her his handkerchief and she wiped her glistening lashes, being careful not to redden her eyes. "I can forget it ever happened," she said. "I only remembered so I could tell you."

"I'm going to forget that you told me," Randy said.

Hazel threw her arms around his neck and kissed him, pushing him back onto the couch. "I could forgive you anything," she whispered drowsily in his ear.

She had got off lighter than she had expected. She had not believed he would break it off, but she had thought he might become angry and make a scene, or demand the same privilege as her first lover. It occurred to her that perhaps he had something in his own past that needed forgiving.

"Is there anything you want to tell me?" she asked.

"No," he said, gently freeing himself.

"You don't think I can be as forgiving as you," she pouted.

"There's nothing to tell," he said.

"You were in the service. Surely you did some things. . . ."

"Nothing like that."

She eyed him suspiciously, unable to decide whether he had done something too terrible to confess or nothing at all. Reluctantly she decided on the latter.

"You've never been in love before, have you?" she asked. Her tone was faintly superior and Randy felt intimidated.

"Yes, there was one time."

"You can tell me about it. I won't mind," she said generously.

"There's nothing to tell and it was a long time ago."

Randy was sorry he had mentioned it. He did not want to tell. It was not much of a story, and something like it had happened to most people many times. But it had happened to Randy only once. It was his fondest memory when he wanted to think of time, and love, and what might have been.

Randy sat very still hoping she would change the subject, but she did not. She was curious and not a little amused. She turned toward him so that her heavy breast pressed against his shoulder, and laid her hand on his. "It's only fair," she said. "I told you my most important secret. You can tell me about your little romance."

Reluctantly, Randy told his story. After completion of boot training, he had gone home on leave during the Christmas season. It had been the worst experience of his life. The town was smaller and duller than he had remembered, his friends were either married or gone, his girl friend was busy with high school athletes, and his parents were continually embarrassed because they kept forgetting that he was back home again. He had reported to Camp Pendleton in relief and despair. It was New Year's Eve and to his surprise he had been given a 71-hour pass. He ran into a man named Cook from his boot platoon who had reported in at the same time, and together, they had gone to Los Angeles. He and Cook, lonely in the crowd, walked about the streets thinking of home and girls.

Then he saw her. She was walking toward him, seeming totally apart from the crowd. He could not remember what she looked like, except that she was beautiful with dark hair and eyes, and that her deeply tanned face was flushed with excitement. When she passed him, he fell in beside her. He did not remember what he had said, but he believed he had talked to her without brashness or silliness, and that she had listened, although she did not look at him. When they reached the corner, the stream of people was so heavy going the opposite way, that he had guided her through. Across the street, he had guided her into a drugstore. They went into the basement, and since all the booths were full, they sat at a long counter. For the first time he realized that the girl had two companions, and that Cook was with one of them, and some marine neither of them knew was with the other. He was annoyed to see Cook and the other Marine. This had been something unique. It was the meeting of two young people who, because they were young and healthy and innocent, wanted against all reason to be in the presence of each other at a time of joy. It was one of those meetings that happen without reason and haunt you forever after with ideas of fate and destiny. Cook and the other Marine had made it commonplace and possible.

They had ordered coffee and doughnuts, and had talked. Her name was Joyce something and she was from Alhambra. He could never remember what her last name was, but to him, it had sounded foreign.

"I'm from Chillicothe," he said.

"Ohio?"

"No, Texas."

She looked at him closely. "I never heard of it," she said.

"It's a small town," he admitted. "My father was the first person ever born there."

"Does your father own a ranch?"

"No, he's a farmer. Wheat mostly."

"Can you ride a horse?"

"No," he admitted reluctantly. "But I can drive a tractor."

"It's Illinois, isn't it?"

"What?"

"You're from Chillicothe, Illinois."

"No, it's Texas. Can't you tell by the way I talk?"

"Maybe it's Missouri you're from," she said.

Laughing, he shook his head. "If you were from Illinois, I'd know what you were like," she said. "But I think anyone from Chillicothe, Texas can be anything they want to be."

They walked through the streets pristine and inviolable, throwing streamers and confetti and singing the Marine Corps Hymn and the Eyes of Texas. The crowds on the sidewalks had overflowed into the street and all traffic had stopped. They did the foolish things that are excusable only in the very young who believe the world loves them because they are happy and capable of love. Cook and the other

Marine and the two girls followed them, but they did not notice.

"Are you going to Korea?" she asked.

"Soon."

"My brother is in the Marines," she said, and he was glad. It made their relationship seem secure and predestined. Her brother might be his friend. Their hands tightened.

Horns and bells and cheering announced the New Year. They stopped and she turned to him. He kissed her, oblivious to the crowd, and then he perfunctorily kissed the other two girls, and he had been kissed by other women who crowded the street.

And when Cook said, "I like the way your girl kisses; mine kisses with her mouth open," he had been glad.

Slowly the crowds began thinning out and they had walked along hand in hand through the paper-littered streets.

"Where can I find you again?" he asked.

"Here," she said, and he had looked up at the large department store, memorizing the name.

They found their way into a bus station where they ordered hamburgers and coffee. Randy was annoyed by a shriveled, painted woman of forty, obviously drunk, who tried to square dance with him. Joyce had laughed.

The girls had come to see the Rose Parade so they agreed to go together. Randy and Joyce wanted to walk. The others thought it was too far, but followed them anyway.

When they came out of the bus station, the papers were blowing softly and silently down the deserted streets, and they believed it had never happened anywhere else at any other time. They walked through the blowing papers feeling lovely, and alone, and lost.

The night was cool and damp and they stopped frequently to sit huddled together on the curb to rest. Toward morning, they caught a bus to Pasadena, and Joyce slept on his arm. They found a place where they could see the parade, and the three marines elbowed a place for the girls to stand, and then went for coffee and sandwiches.

The parade was long, and tiresome, and thrilling. They watched for hours standing close together and calling each other's attention to obvious details, until the parade became a blur of color and faces. At the end of the parade, suffocated by the crowd, they sat down on the curb and waited for the streets to clear.

Again they walked through the paper-littered streets, looking for a place that was dark and quiet, until they found a restaurant where they could sit at a table under a little thatched roof with only candles for light. They were too exhausted to eat much, but Joyce clung to his arm.

They walked outside and tried to say goodbye, timid with indiscretion. The shyness that should have characterized their meeting was reserved for their parting. Their meeting had been outside their experience, and now they did not know how to put it on a regular, secure footing. Randy took her in his arms and kissed her goodbye.

"Are you really from Chillicothe?" she asked with her head buried in his shoulder.

"Yes."

They put the dazed and exhausted girls into a cab. As he closed the door and stepped back, Joyce burst into tears. She shouted something to him through the back glass as the cab pulled away but he could not understand it . . .

When he returned to the base, he had been assigned to a replacement draft, and for three weeks he was unable to get away. On his first pass he returned to Los Angeles and looked for the department store. He went through it department by department, but she was not there and no one remembered her. Until he shipped out, he spent every weekend liberty walking the streets of Los Angeles, or standing under a street light watching the papers blowing lazily down the street, in the idiotic dream of finding her the way he found her the first time, coming to him from out of the crowd. He never saw her again.

"Is that all?" Hazel asked. Her attention had wandered and she had been startled by the sudden ending.

"I guess so," he said. "You know Cook was killed in Korea." He leaned his head against her shoulder and began to relax. "It was just a memory. Just something I thought of," he said.

"It's the kind of thing that happens every New Year's in a big city," she said, a little disappointed.

I wonder what would have come of it, he thought. What if her folks had been Italian, or Jewish, or Catholic? Would that have made a difference? What if her father had sold vegetables on the street, or run a tavern? What if she had wanted to live in California? I probably never would have married her, he thought. It would never be the same again.

It was one of those one-time things that never happen twice. Things are always the same with Hazel, he thought. No big surprises. I wonder if I should marry Hazel, he thought.

He looked up at Hazel and saw that her face was soft and there were traces of a smile on her lips. But Hazel was not thinking of Randy. She was thinking of strong rough hands and powerful arms that tore and crushed and caressed at the same time.

The boy from Chillicothe was thinking of the streets of Los Angeles at three o'clock in the morning when their lips met.

WAITING FOR THE POSTMAN

As a child I dreamed of the moon and was content to wait for the postman. It was that blue-moon time between Hiroshima and Korea when we owned the world and believed the world worth having.

I was a serious youth, tall with ambition, thin with profession, my craftless face dominated by the bright red hair that set its color scheme, and pale gray eyes that looked out upon a reasonable if untempered world. No matter, I disavowed comets and concerned myself with conquering high school, and earning my place in the world. I would learn that peace cannot be won but must be conceded before I would discover that some places cannot be earned but must be granted.

One of the places I wanted to earn was the central spot in Joy McKinney's heart. Joy had a flawless delicate face that made cannibals of my eyes, long silky hair that she tossed impatiently, lashing my libido, a slender almost boyish figure that drove stakes into my heart, and soft green eyes that twisted a knife in what I usually referred to as my stomach.

Joy also had an impudent disregard for convention that made cowards of us all, except Vivian Whatley who was conventional All-American small town male except for his first name. Vivian, whose mother had more pretension than learning, was crude, arrogant, curly haired, and class favorite. He peeled scabs from his gallant elbows to attract Joy's attention and treated her like she wasn't class secretary, Homecoming Queen, and F.F.A. Sweetheart.

"Hey, Joy, you got a butt like a little boy."

Joy tossed her hair and examined her tight-skirted hip. "Will likes my butt," she said, showing me her little boy's butt. "Don't you, Will?"

I ducked my head and hurried away, my shining face betraying my pretension that I hadn't heard her. It hurt that Vivian had made me look foolish, but it hurt more that he had made Joy look frivolous. I didn't believe that she would ultimately choose Vivian over me; she was too fine a person for that. But quality was subtle and took time to reveal itself and in the meantime Vivian might infect her with his own vulgarity.

For days I plotted ways to take vengeance on Vivian while demonstrating to Joy the kind of behavior that was expected of a young lady. Usually, in the imagined scenarios, I hit Vivian in the sneering lips, knocking him down in front of an astonished Joy. "That's for saying Joy's butt is small," I said, as he looked up at me in fear and respect through his curly locks. "I happen to like it."

Then with all the arrogance of Vivian Whatley, I pulled Joy roughly to me, kissed her forcefully on the lips, squeezed her ass—Vivian's crude jest had not only infuriated me, it had focalized my febrile imagination—then turned and strode away, leaving her speechless.

Although I believed that with right on my side I could whip Vivian, I never put my plan into effect because I couldn't convince myself that I could astonish Joy, leave her speechless, or say "butt" in front of her. Also I thought the message might be enigmatic.

I eschewed vengeance, trusting that justice would prevail. I would work hard, harder than anyone, and Joy, along with other rewards, would be mine. I wrote extra papers to gain the respect of my teachers who fled to the faculty lounge to avoid me. I worked after football practice to impress the coach who was in the locker room asking Vivian about the high school girls. I wrote thoughtful letters on meaningful issues to the school paper to attract the admiration of my peers who seemed interested only in Anne Tooley's column of original rumor. No one was less impressed than Joy.

"Don't you ever do anything but write?" she asked, catching me writing an essay on "The Causes of Poverty and Social Distress."

Her tone of voice, the way she wrinkled her nose when she said "write" should have been warning enough. "I have to write every day if I'm going to be a writer," I said, staring into space both to look earnest and to avoid looking into those soft green eyes that could turn my tongue into an ill-bred dog that rolled over and played dead.

After a distinguished college career, I planned to get a job with a newspaper, and win a Pulitzer by the time I was twenty-four. In my mind she would wait that long. "I wanted you to have this," I'd say, handing her my Pulitzer. "Oh Will," she'd say, her green eyes swimming with love and admiration. "And this," I'd say, handing her a tiny box concealing an enormous diamond ring. "Oh Will," she'd say. "Oh my God."

"Why do you want to be a writer?" she asked.

Instead of confessing that I wanted to be a writer so that I could compose sonnets in praise of her, I elaborated the difficulty of the feat I was attempting, the achievement that was going to steal her heart. "I have to make good grades so I can go to college, and if I work really hard, I'll get to be on the college paper, and by my senior year, if I work harder than anybody, I might get to be editor of the college paper, and some real newspaper is bound to notice me and offer me a job, and although I'll have to start at the bottom, if I really work—"

"That is so damn boring." Joy was the only girl in the school who cursed in front of boys. In my fantasies she always swore off swearing out of love for me. "I hate boring people."

My heart sank at that. It had not occurred to me that a prospective Pulitzer winner could be boring. In my dreams she saw me as terribly dedicated, if not profound. "Don't you ever think of anything besides work?"

Of course I thought of other things. I thought of her all the time. I thought of her rapture when she saw the Pulitzer, her excitement when she saw the diamond. I thought of her slipping away to some secret place to read "The Causes of

Crime and Social Unrest." I thought of her tender glances intended only for me, her look of adoration intended for the whole world to see. But I guarded that secret with my life. "I read a lot," I said.

For a moment I thought she was going to find that boring, too, but it seemed to tempt her curiosity if not her admiration. "Have you read *The House of Seven Gables*?"

"Sure," I said. A book report was due the next day. "Haven't you?"

"It's so damn dull. I hate dull books."

"What about your book report?"

"I hate doing everything I'm told to do. That's so damn weak and I hate weakness."

She said no more, nor did she need to. I could not bear the thought of her failure. She wouldn't be in my class anymore. I would hardly see her. I learned the geography of Korea before I learned that girls like Joy did not fail at what others could do for them. "I could help you write it," I said, hoping that wasn't weak. A Pulitzer was several years away. Maybe I could capture her heart with my writing skill now.

I wrote the report for her and after that we often studied together. Which meant that I wrote reports and made crib notes for her while she thumbed through magazines, played records, and interrupted my thoughts by asking my opinion of different girls in our class.

She seemed disappointed in my answers—I thought they were all nice—and eventually she asked what I thought of her. I, who had written "The Causes of War and Social

Disorder," could not say what I thought of the person I thought of all the time. I could not describe the music I heard when I said her name, or the enchantment I got from hours spent writing her name. There were no words to tell how when I looked into her eyes something in me was lost and found, died and was reborn, fell into nothing and sprang into sunlight; that I lived only to see her, yet sometimes ran away to avoid the intense pleasure and pain that seeing her brought to what I usually thought of as my heart.

"I think you are very nice," I said.

"You are so damn dull," she said, tossing her hair. "I don't know what I like about you."

I would realize that I need not win a Pulitzer to win a girl's heart before I realized that I need not have grappled for slippery words to describe untouchable feelings. It would have been sufficient to have said I thought Joy was the prettiest girl in school.

I was not only dull I was stupid. I thought Joy suffered my presence only to avoid school chores that were even drearier than I. I did her work quickly, trying to inflict myself upon her as little as possible.

"Don't you ever want to do anything with me but study?" she asked one day in exasperation.

I stammered, my ears burning, because I didn't know what she meant but I knew all too vividly what I wanted to do with her. I wanted to adore her, to ravish her, to protect her from an unworthy world, to stroke her little boy's butt, to worship her eyes, to fondle her breasts, to adore her lips, to lick her fingers. . . .

"What?" she persisted. "What do you want to do with me?"

"I want to take you to the basketball game," I said.

"Pick me up at seven."

It wasn't until I heard an editor say, "We get more good stories than we can use—but leave it if that's what makes you happy," that I understood Joy's inflection, composed of equal parts of vexation and resignation.

My dreams had come true and I had never been unhappier. I was going to spend an evening with the person I wanted to spend every minute of my life with and I was terrified she would discover how weak and boring I really was. Why hadn't I kept my mouth shut and won her with my prose style?

I arrived at her house twenty minutes early, although I knew that was weak, and waited with her mother who entertained me with stories of Joy's admirers. I was someone Joy studied with.

"Will is taking me to the basketball game," Joy said, when she appeared, ten minutes late. "Aren't you, Will?"

"Yes."

"Oh, that's nice. Will you be late coming home?"

"Will we be late coming home?" Joy asked.

"No."

At the basketball game I tried to please her by pointing out how well Vivian was playing. Vivian was not only our best football player, he was our best basketball player. I did not resent this, I only thought that the other students, like myself, should recognize that this was a transitory distinction, while computational and verbal skills were of lasting value.

I believe I pointed this out to Joy while Vivian led the team to a one-point victory over our arch rival. I believe that while Vivian was sinking the free throw that assured our victory, I accused him of being ephemeral.

Joy did not seem bored with my judicial analysis—praising Vivian's skills while insisting that those skills were without worth. What displeased her was my oration at her doorstep.

"Joy, I know that some boys expect a kiss just because they take a girl to a basketball game and buy her a hamburger and Coke. But I'm not like that. I don't want you to do anything you don't want to do. I would like to kiss you but I'm not going to unless you tell me that you want me to. And I promise that I will never tell anybody. The decision is up to you."

It was a speech I had worked on for hours and carefully memorized. I thought it would prove that I was not like the other boys she knew. Although I began to have misgivings as the time to deliver the speech drew near, I cleared my throat, licked my lips, and made a good beginning. I never got to finish it because Joy slammed the door in my face shortly after "basketball."

For the next few days I avoided Joy so that I would not know she was trying to avoid me. It was weak, but my weakness had been confirmed and her disaffection had not. I wanted to hold that information in abeyance until I could reestablish my worth with the honors that were due me.

Despite my extra reports and my letters to the editor, Hooper Byars, who owned a camera, was appointed editor of the paper. Because of his ephemeral skills, Vivian Whatley was elected senior class president, although he claimed he didn't want it. "Why don't you vote for Will, he wants it," Vivian said magnanimously.

And despite my extra hours after football practice, I watched Vivian called to the stage of the auditorium to be awarded a starred, striped, monogrammed jacket while I stood with fifteen others to be awarded a silver football charm as our reward for attending workouts.

I was able to stand at a bar with newfound friends and laugh at alimony before I was able to laugh at what that coat represented to me. It was clear to me that life's rewards were not earned by those who contended for them but were gifts to those who were chosen. It was also clear to me that I had not been chosen.

I hated that silver football that stamped me as ordinary. Why I took it to Joy is no more puzzling than why I turned to my wife when I did not get the award that would have vindicated my moodiness and obsession with work that left her either wounded or alone.

Perhaps it was a desire to punish myself for believing that by an act of will I could make myself other than ordinary. Or maybe having failed to win the approval of those I had to please in order to get the prize, I tried to find approval in the arms of the one I loved.

"I'm sorry," she said. "I know how hard you worked." At last there was someone who understood. No wonder I loved her. "Awards are so damned ephemeral." I forgave her the plagiarism. "You are the only person in this school I truly admire."

The world had no prize that could match finding admiration in her eyes. I was special. I was one of those life favored. I was a winner. In my life there has always been a fine line between hapless and smug.

Joy led me to the couch, sat down beside me, and put her arms around me. She smoothed my hair and kissed my forehead. "Poor Will," she said. "People are so damn stupid they can't see how damn fine he is." That's when I discovered the way to a woman's heart was to be found wanting.

I sought Joy's lips and found them. I sought her breasts. They were mine to hold. I sought her respect. "Next year I'm going to work twice as hard. I'm going to prove how wrong they were."

That's when I learned the way out of a woman's heart was to continue wanting after being found.

"You are so damn dumb," she said. "You're not going to go through that again, are you?"

I tried to explain why I had to persist. I had turned to her not just to declare failure but to pledge the honors I was going to lay at her feet. I was explaining that I was willing to work twice as hard as anyone else because I wanted something worthy to give her, when I saw the coat folded neatly over a chair.

She had already been offered more than I could promise. Vivian's coat was embellished with stripes for the years he had played, stars for being captain, patches for All-

District and All-State.

I was unable to take my eyes off the coat, folded carefully, placed scrupulously over the back of a chair. One of us was out of place.

"I know it isn't important to you, Will, and that's right for you. But it's something I've always wanted, and it's something you can never give me. It's not your fault, you just want other, better, things. They're right for you, but they're not right for me, and I don't want to have to make the effort any more."

I left the house with nothing but the knowledge that the moon is not a star. I didn't see Vivian or Joy again until after Korea, college, a job on a newspaper, and marriage to an artless girl who wanted to give me everything she wanted.

Joy had married a truck driver and after two children had left him for a pharmacist twelve years her senior who sent the kids to summer camp and dressed her not wisely but too well. "Do you think Anne really had a crush on Hooper Byars?" she asked at the reunion. "Or did she just go with him to get her picture in the school paper?"

Vivian had not only failed at college, he had failed to make the freshman football team and had become a barber. He remembered that I had been on the receiving end of a thirty-eight-yard touchdown pass. The fact that it was one of three passes I caught in high school football, and that the game had been won in the first quarter, was not as important to him as the fact that he had thrown the ball.

I left her house with nothing but the knowledge that the moon has its seasons. I still dream of the moon. I wait for the postman who sometimes brings a rejection slip, sometimes a postcard from the children. I, who was the first to recognize that life's rewards are ephemeral, have become the last to give up waiting for the postman.

THE KILLER

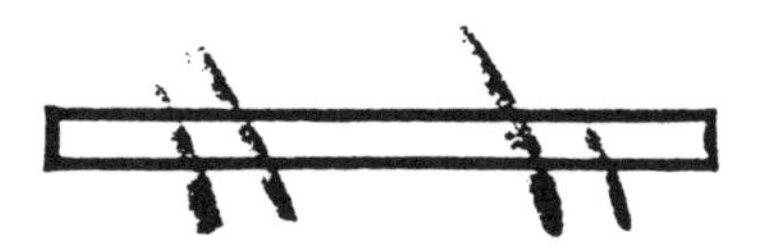

It was a standard patrol. Single file through the wire at first light. Lock and load weapons. Single file down the trail under trees hung with burned out flares. String out along the ravine around the crater left by a mine. Single file across the rock bottomed creek. Fan out through the ville and check the hootches. Single file through the bamboo. Spread out across the paddy. Single file through the treeline. Fan out through the ville and check the hootches. Single file across the swift, treacherous river. Spread out through the grass in the valley of the wind. Close in around the ville and check the hootches. Two files around the hill. Two trails through the bush. Link up under the Aleppo pines. Single file back to the wire. Unload weapons. Single file through the wire before dusk. Check in grenades.

It was routine except that this day one of the men killed a Viet Cong sniper. Sherrill O'Connell, reporter for *Real* magazine, interviewed him when they returned to the base camp. The killer was sitting with his helmet and rifle between his knees, his back against a sandbagged bunker, a cigarette in one hand, a beer in the other. Sweat clung to his forehead and dripped from his smooth chin. O'Connell made a note that he was animated, exhausted, bewildered.

"God damn," he said.

O'Connell sat beside him. "What's your name?"

"You going to write about me?"

"Maybe."

"The Army calls me Cletus Harvey but don't write that. Write me down as Spike." O'Connell made a note. "And don't say I'm skinny. My momma don't like that. Say I am wiry. And don't make me out baby-faced neither."

O'Connell wrote ". . . the look of a little boy who has just been bitten by his own dog."

"Where are you from, Spike?"

"Texas. Don't say I'm a Rexall. Say I am a real cowboy."

Sherrill wrote down "cowboy." "What did you do in Texas?"

"Went to school. Played second base. Worked in a feed store. Don't say I swept floors."

Sherrill scratched through "cowboy." "I understand you killed a man today."

"I wasted a Charlie. Hit him right in the neck." He pointed at a spot just below the corner of his jaw. "He didn't even scream. Blew the whole side of his head out."

"Was it your first kill?"

"Hey, man, this was my first patrol. My first shot. Hey, I ain't even been shot at yet. I fired the first shot I heard. The first gook I seen I killed. Hey, if I kill somebody every day I'll kill three hundred and . . . God damn."

"How long have you been here?"

"I just got here yesterday, man. The day before that I was in Ban Me Thout. The day before that I was in Saigon.

And the day . . . or the night . . . hey, how long was we in Saigon? Anyway, the day before that I was in . . . I was in . . . fucking California. And the day before that, man, I was home. That's . . . let's see, that's one, two, three, four days. If I get one every three days I'll have a hundred by the time I DEROS. A hundred and twenty . . . one or two. Jesus. God damn."

"What was the patrol like?"

"They all said it was a slide. They said we was skating. This was just to get me ready for the humping I'll have to do later on. But man, it kicked my ass. I ain't never been so hot. I could hear my heart beating in my head. 'How far we come?' I said. 'Oh, about ten klicks.' Ten klicks. Hell, I can run ten klicks."

"When did you first see the enemy?"

"We was taking a break, all crapped out along the trail in this little clearing, and I walked back in the bush to drain my lizard, and I seen this dude with a rifle. He wasn't much farther than that piss tube over there. Hey, I said, because I didn't want to shoot no friendly. I didn't even know what the enemy look like. Then he aimed his rifle at somebody and there wasn't nobody for him to shoot at but us, so I shot him. Wet on myself, too, but I had my pecker out. Hit him right in the neck. He just stood there and . . . blew out the whole side of his head. Don't say I pissed on myself."

"Wet his pants," O'Connell wrote in his notebook. "How do you feel about killing a man?"

The killer threw away his cigarette and lighted another one. O'Connell made a note that he was wearing a high school ring. It looked new. "I was doing my job. I probably saved somebody's life. He was the enemy and I'm doing what I'm supposed to do. I don't feel . . ." He wet the corners of his mouth with his tongue. "I mean, I'm sorry that he had to die, but he didn't have to point that rifle."

"Do you feel you did something wrong?"

"I reckon I could have told him to *chieu hoi.*"

"You have no feelings of guilt?"

"Just say . . . say the best man won," the killer said, showing his teeth.

Sherrill wrote, "Best man won, he said with a smile," and closed his notebook. Others had slowly gathered to watch the interview and when it was over they closed in to congratulate the killer. "Don't tell my mama I did something wrong," he said to O'Connell. "I promised her I wouldn't shoot nobody."

Sherrill made a note to call the story "The Promise."

"Hey, blood brother, heard you zapped a cong," said a huge black machine gunner, slapping hands with the killer and going through an elaborate handshake. O'Connell noted he was the kind of black one had rather meet in a living room than in an alley.

"Killed the motherfucker with my first shot. Hit him right in the neck," he said, pointing a finger at the spot. "I only been here a week. If I kill somebody ever week . . . fifty-two people. Minus one for R&R."

"There it is. Come the revolution we gonna be needing you."

"Real fine, soldier," said a pimple-faced lieutenant. He

looked to Sherrill like the kind of man who in high school went by the nickname "crater face," and was remembered for dropping his pencil in study hall so he could bend over and look up the girls' miniskirts. "You saved my life. They always go for your officers first. Thank you muchly."

"I hit him high. Right in the neck." He pointed at the spot. "I was aiming at his chest."

"You saved your leader and now he is going to look after you."

"Thank you, sir."

"There is no color between us. Check it, trooper. No color."

"Yes, sir."

"That's affirm."

"God bless you, son," said the deep-throated, short-legged chaplain. He seemed to be all head and chest, a man who spent more time studying speech than theology. "Sometimes it is tragically necessary to kill in the defense of one's life or family or national honor."

"Yes, sir."

"Are you a Christian, my son?"

"Yes, sir," the killer said, making the sign of the cross.

"Are you Catholic; there's a Catholic chaplain."

"No, sir, I'm Baptist. I don't know why I did that."

"Well, God forgives Baptist boys for killing the enemy. Have you asked for forgiveness?"

"I ain't had much time."

"Then get your sierra together, soldier," the chaplain said in an attempt at jovial amiability. "Thank God for preserving your life to this very hour. And pray for free world forces everywhere."

Some of the men prayed and others looked around in embarrassment. One of them, wearing the crisp new uniform and the white, unlined face of a newby, prayed with a fervency matched only by the intensity with which he picked his nose. "Hear the prayer of thy children, O God," the chaplain prayed. "Make us strong that we may continue thy fight against the forces of godless communism. We pray in the name of Jesus who died for us all. Amen."

"I hear you're not cherry any more," said a joyless kid with three hundred days behind his eyes. He had a grenade pin in his bush hat, love beads around his neck, jungle sores on his arms, and Ho Chi Minh sandals on his feet. He looked like a supposer to O'Connell, a man who chewed his mind instead of his nails. O'Connell put him down as a man who would always have a month to go. Even if he got back to the world his tour would never be over.

"I saw him before he saw me. Hit him right in the neck."

"I guess somebody had to kill the old fart. That old papasan has been taking shots at us ever since I been here. He never hit anybody though. Glad it was you that got him and not me."

"You think I shouldn't have shot him? What am I supposed to do, let him shoot my buddies? How am I supposed to know who to shoot and who not to shoot?"

"Sorry about that, hero," he sneered.

"What the fuck do you want?" the killer said. "I just got here."

"Hey tiger, got you a dink," said the sergeant, a hulking lifer who had more malice for his own men than for the enemy. "Going to get some more tomorrow, right?"

"God damn. Right," the killer said, wiping his mouth with the back of his hand and swallowing whatever was welling in his throat. "Kill the motherfuckers."

"Outstanding. The lieutenant said you didn't have to go out tomorrow if you didn't want to, but I knew a blood like you would want to get with the program. Tomorrow we're going into Indian country. And some of you fuckers are going to die."

"God damn."

Everybody had left except O'Connell and the fervent nose picker who had been hanging around the edge of the crowd. He squatted beside the killer. "What's it like?" he asked. "I'm going out on my first patrol tomorrow."

The killer leaned back against the sandbags and looked up at the first stars. "Jesus God, I'm going out tomorrow. Three hundred and sixty days to go. Ain't no way."

"Were you scared when you went out? I got to know."

"Don't say I was scared. Say I was . . . say I was thoughtful."

"What's it like to kill somebody?"

"I seen him and I shot him. Blew out the whole side of his head. For a minute he just stood there. Like he was surprised. He just stood there and I says, son of a bitch I done a bad thing. I thought he was going to turn and look at me like I done a bad thing. I seen stuff blow out the side of his head but he didn't fall and I says, son of a bitch I missed him. And I was scared. And glad. And awful. And then his rifle dropped and he just . . . he didn't fall, man, he just sank. He just sank straight down. I heard him, man. I heard him snapping his teeth."

"What if I can't do it. What if somebody gets killed because I can't do it?"

"I heard him snapping his teeth. And I saw his face. He was real, man. He was . . . my daddy killed people in Germany. But I didn't know they were real. They were Nazis."

For a while no one spoke. The mosquitoes came in waves and behind them a mortar coughed. A flare popped high in the sky and hung sizzling beneath its tiny parachute, blotting out the stars.

"You going to chow?" the nose picker asked.

"I ain't hungry," the killer said.

"You coming to the hootch?"

"I may lay out for a while. I don't want to hear nobody snoring and clicking their teeth."

The newby left to find his own accommodations. The killer lighted a cigarette and blew smoke upward at the sky. "He was just a little guy," he said. "Just a little old man."

O'Connell waited, offering himself to the mosquitoes as a kind of penance.

"If you write about me, say I wish it had been somebody else," the killer said. "Say I wish it had been folks I ain't even heard of."

THE FEELINGS OF THE DEAD

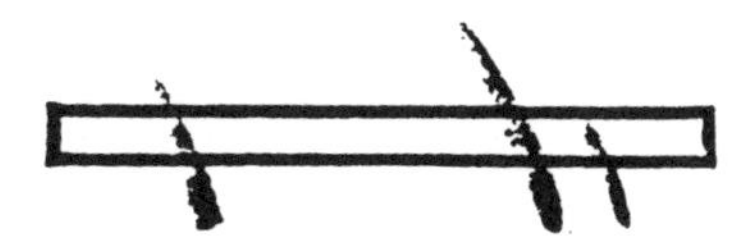

The sun was hot and inescapable. The landing zone was on a barren limestone ridge with wooded peaks rising above it. On another ridge an artillery battery was digging in, one of the guns already firing, the bang and echoing thump chasing each other through the valleys. Smoke rose from one of the peaks. Far below was the muddy Song Cha Nang and more smoke. The helicopters that had spent the morning bringing troops were returning to remove the bodies.

Five men struggled up the hill carrying a sixth in a poncho. It would have been easier for one of them to carry the packs and rifles, leaving four to carry the dead man, but they all had a hand on the improvised litter. The faces of the five were drawn and grimy and they stumbled with fatigue as they heaved their burden past the neat row of bodies on the LZ. "Put him there on the end," said one of the sweating, cursing men who were loading the bodies into a helicopter.

"We'll take care of this one," said the black man carrying the foot of the poncho. They carried the dead man well past the LZ to a level bit of ground where they dropped him without ceremony, threw the corners of the poncho over him, and sat down beside him. The helicopter lifted off, stirring up a mini-tornado of dust, and they shut their eyes and bowed their heads over the dead man.

Beneath their helmets, uniforms, and the dust and grime of battle, there was little to distinguish between them. One was black, one white although at the moment his face was red from exertion and sunburn. One wore love beads and had written "love child not war child" on the cover of his helmet. One was thick, droopy-eyed, with a tattoo on his muscular arm: Death Before Dishonor. One was nondescript.

When the noise and violence had passed, they opened their eyes. They did not look at the dead man. They did not look at anything. "How far do you think we come?" asked the black man who had a naturally upturned mouth that made him look cheerful despite his weariness.

"Same distance we got to go back," said whitey, whose white eyebrows and the long white hairs on his upper lip stood in contrast to his red, peeling face.

"Fuck it," said love child. "It ain't real."

"Who was the poor bastard anyway?" asked death-before-dishonor.

"Some fucking Polack from Oklahoma."

"How could he be a fucking Polack if he was from Oklahoma?" asked nondescript. There may have been a trace of L.A. in his voice. Lower Alabama.

"You think you have to be an Indian to be from Oklahoma, shithead?" asked death-before-dishonor. "When was he hit?"

"He got zapped when we crossed that ravine this morning," said whitey. "Same time as doc and that new kid. Hey, maybe he didn't finish his smokes." He pulled back the poncho and started going through the dead man's pockets. "Fucking Salems," whitey said. "Nobody but a fucking Polack would smoke these fucking Salems."

"Lay off the fucking Polacks," said love child.

"That ain't right," said death-before-dishonor. "Taking things from a dead man."

"He don't have no more use for them," said the black.

"If it was me I'd want you guys to have them," said nondescript, wetting his lips.

"Fuck it," said love child. "It ain't real."

Whitey took a cigarette and passed the pack around. "His name is Kersnowski," he said, examining the dog tags. "Hey, he's a fucking Protestant."

"How can he be a fucking Protestant if he's a fucking Polack?" asked nondescript.

"Lay off the fucking Protestants," said love child.

Another helicopter came in and the conversation stopped as they ducked away from the noise and dirt. On takeoff, the rotor wash blew the poncho off the dead man, exposing the sunken eyes and gaping mouth. "Charlie did a J.O.B. on him," death-before-dishonor said in awe.

"Don't he look young," said whitey, covering him again. Whitey looked both eighteen and forty.

"How old are you?" asked the black man, smiling his perpetual smile.

"Eighteen, but I been here nine months." He took off his helmet and examined the numbers written on the cloth cover. Those above seventy-three had been marked out. "Seventy-three more days," he said. "Seventy-two and a wake-up."

"Seventy-one not counting today," said nondescript.

"Today counts until tomorrow," said whitey. "I don't mark off a day until it's light enough to see green. That's how I know I ain't in hell."

"I thought this was hell," said death-before-dishonor.

"If you die it's hell," said nondescript.

"If you don't die it's hell," said whitey.

"Fuck it," said love child. "It ain't real."

"Hey man, don't kid about hell around a dead man," said the black man.

Another helicopter came in, spraying them with grit, whipping the row of rubberized ponchos, making flags of the tags attached to the boots of the dead. "Did you talk to him?" asked death-before-dishonor when the helicopter was gone.

"Just when he was dying," whitey said.

"What did he say?"

"He said mama. What the fuck do you think he said? He said doc, doc, I'm dying. He said Jesus, save me."

"Why did he say Jesus if he's a fucking Protestant?" asked nondescript.

"Fucking Protestants believe in Jesus, for christsake," said the black man.

"Lay off the fucking Protestants," said love child.

"It's the fucking Jews who don't believe in Jesus," said nondescript, correcting himself.

"Lay off the fucking Jews," said love child.

"Are you a fucking Protestant or a fucking Jew?" asked nondescript.

"What the fuck is it to you?" asked love child.

"It ain't nothing big, pecker breath."

"Then shut the fuck up, motherfucker."

"The only mother I ever fucked was yours, fart face."

"My mother is fucking dead, maggot breath. You fucked a fucking corpse."

"No wonder she was a dry fuck. Jesus, if she hadn't been so ugly I would have kissed her."

"Does that fucking Polack have another fucking Salem?" asked the black.

"Fucking Polacks are queer for fucking Salems," said whitey, going through the dead man's pockets again.

"At least he's going home," said love child.

"Fuck that shit. I'd rather stay here the rest of my life than go home like that," said the black.

"If you stay here the rest of your life you will go home like that, dumbass," said nondescript.

"Stick it up your ass," said the black.

"I can't. When it's hard it won't bend, and when it's soft it won't go in."

"When was you ever hard?" asked death-before-dishonor.

"The last time I saw you eat a banana, cunt face."

"You ain't seen nothing until you've seen a fucking brother eat a banana," said death-before-dishonor.

"Lay off the—"

"Hey man," the black said, putting a hand on love child's shoulder. "This one's on me. Lay off the fucking brothers," he said to death-before-dishonor. This time the smile was grim and deliberate.

"Lay chili," said whitey. "We got a dead man here."

"What are you going to do when you get home?" asked nondescript.

"I'm going to keep my head down. Them fucking pacifists back in the world will blow you away for being in fucking 'Nam," said whitey.

"Lay off the fucking pacifists," said love child.

"Not me," said the black. "I'm going to lay the Statue of Liberty. I can't wait to get my teeth into them tits."

"There it is," said nondescript. "What I would give for some pussy."

"What I would give for some pot," said love child. "Mary Jo Warner." He tasted the words with his mouth.

"What I would give for tomorrow," said whitey. "Seventy-one days and a wake-up."

"Hey, I'm a one-digit midget," said nondescript. "Nine more to go."

"Yeah, nine months," said whitey.

"I don't think you ought to talk about going home in front of a man who is done gone," said love child.

"I don't think you ought to talk about going home in front of a long-timer like me," said death-before-dishonor. "I still got ten months to go."

"Jesus," said nondescript. "That's three hundred days."

"Fuck it," said love child. "It don't mean nothing."

"Don't start counting before you get to a hundred," said whitey.

"How the fuck do you know when you get to a hundred if you don't count," said nondescript.

"Hey. You men," someone shouted from the LZ. An officer had come in on one of the helicopters, fresh from Chu Lai. His uniform was not only clean and starched, it was new, his boots polished. "We'll take care of the K.I.A. You get back to your squad."

Nondescript rose slowly to his feet, raising his rifle at the same time, but not exactly pointing it. "This is our squad," he said. "We didn't even get to say goodbye to the others, and we're going to see this one off."

The officer glared, opened his mouth, hands on hips. Nondescript's rifle moved slightly in his direction. "I want that corpse on the next chopper," the officer said, then turned and walked away.

"Fucking lifers, they got no respect for the feelings of the dead," said nondescript.

"Lay off the fucking lifers," said love child, but his heart wasn't in it.

"Let's have one last cigarette before we go," said death-before-dishonor.

Whitey uncovered the body and took out the pack. "Last two," he said.

"Leave him one," said death-before-dishonor.

Whitey looked at the circle of faces. The black nodded. Nondescript shrugged. "Fuck it," said love child.

Whitey took out one cigarette and replaced the other in

the dead man's pocket. He lighted the cigarette, took a drag, and passed it around the circle. They could hear the wap wap wap of a helicopter and the officer was glaring at them but no one moved until the cigarette had made its circle back to whitey who field stripped it, sprinkling the tobacco on the ground, rolling the paper into a ball and throwing it away. The filter he slipped into the dead man's pocket with the cigarette pack.

They stood up, picked up the poncho, and braced against the swirling wind and dust, they ran to the settling helicopter and lifted the man aboard. They waited while the working party loaded the helicopter. As it lifted off, they stood at attention, their eyes and mouths tightly closed against the dust, their uniforms flapping in the gale. Then they turned and started downhill under the white and inescapable sun.

Christmas in a Very Small Place

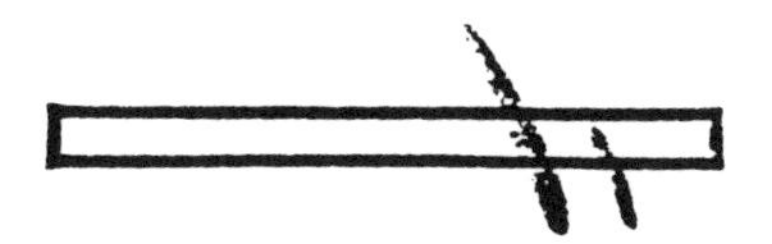

When Newly looked at his watch it wasn't the time he was looking at, or the date. They were of no importance. He was looking at his watch, the new Seiko he had bought only a week ago in the Freedom Hill PX. Already it was grimy and he was worried that staying wet for a year would ruin it. He noticed the date only by accident. December 25. He looked for someone to tell. Ortega seemed to be asleep. "It's Christmas," he said to the old papasan who sat in another corner slowly adding rice straw to a small fire. The papasan smiled and nodded.

Since the Marines had come to the ville the Viet Cong had not come to take rice and young men, but they shot at the Marines in the ville, dropped mortars on it, and set boobytraps along the trails. Since the Marines had come to the ville, the families had been safer, and the threat of violence had been greater. The papasan knew these things the way he knew the monsoon and the mosquitoes, the dry season and the dust. They came when they wished and they were to be endured until they passed. He did not know why the American was excited. He nodded as he always did and smiled for the Americans.

Not satisfied, Newly looked at Ortega again. The squad

had moved three times during the night, in and around the ville. Because they had no barbed wire and no bunkers, and their only support was the artillery at the combat base five miles away, frequent movement was their only security. That and the almost animal awareness some of them had. Ortega had the long, lithe body and the senses of a coyote. He could go to sleep anywhere and be instantly awake.

Newly brushed his hand against the straw side of the hootch and Ortega's eyes opened. "Know what day it is?" Newly asked.

Ortega looked at the months and days he had crossed off the calendar he kept on his helmet. "Twenty-fifth. I'm short as peace," he said. "Fourteen days to go."

"It's Christmas Day."

Ortega shrugged. "Ain't but two days that matter. The day you go on R&R and the day you go home."

Deflated, Newly picked up his rifle and stepped outside into the early morning mist. Mother was conferring with the Popular Forces honcho. Mother, who was built like a dark street corner, big, black and intimidating, was a twenty-one-year-old high school dropout-Marine corporal, who was responsible for the security of the bridge and the road that connected the ville to the market and the Marines to the combat base, five miles and a lifetime away.

Mother was also responsible for the safety of the families in the ville and for training the Popular Forces to defend it. Mother, who had never been anything but unnecessary back in the world, was on his second tour in the ville. He was wearing sandals with his trousers legs rolled up. He had shrapnel wounds in both legs that would not heal because he could not keep them dry.

When Mother and the PF honcho finished talking, Newly said, "It's Christmas Day."

"Damn," Mother said. "That means we won't get a replacement corpsman today." The doc had been wounded the day before in a fight in the cemetery. "They won't send a replacement out here on Christmas. He's in Danang right now, his feet dry, eating turkey."

"Won't we get turkey?" Newly asked.

"Man, what are you talking? Turkey is for pogues in Danang. We'll get turkey when they put it in C-rations. On Thanksgiving we got hamburger patties. On the Corps' birthday we got ice cream. Last Christmas we got roast beef. If we're lucky that's what we'll get today."

"Merry Christmas to you too," Newly said. He was not going to let anyone spoil his Christmas. He went to a hootch and looked in. Dig was sitting on the damp floor cleaning his machine gun. "Hey, Dig, it's Christmas Day."

"It don't mean nothing," Dig said.

"It means there's a truce, don't it?"

"It ain't real," Dig said. "We lost Bear and Lower Alabam the last time we had a truce."

Mother loomed in the doorway of the hootch, holding the radio. "Old man says we only got to pull one patrol today because it's Christmas. Plus an alley cat tonight. I need the machine gun, Dig, and I want you on the radio, Newly Arrived. I want you to get to know every face and hootch in this ville. It's the only way you'll ever know when something's wrong. Let's go, because the jeep driver is bringing roast beef and stewed tomatoes for Christmas dinner, and toys for us to give to the kids."

"It ain't real," Dig said. On an earlier tour Dig had been the only survivor of a platoon ambushed in the Quesons. The experience left him with definite opinions about what was real. "I'm walking but I'm dead," he said. The Marines had sent him back to the world but the world did not conform to his expectations of reality. "You can't do nothing to me but bury me," he said to parents, peers, and protestors who tried to change, honor, or chastise him. "So dig." After three months he asked for Vietnam.

When they stepped outside the hootch, Ortega joined them. "You don't have to go," Mother said. "You're short."

"It's as safe on patrol as it is here," Ortega said. "And it's the only way I got to make the days go faster. Thirteen days and a wake up."

"It don't mean nothing," Dig said. "You think you're going back to the world but it ain't real."

Ignoring him, Ortega took the point. Ortega had the best nose in the squad, only Mother knew the ville better. They slipped along the muddy footpath between the hootches. Mother stopped to bow and speak to the PFs and the peasants, looking into each hootch.

They walked past the garden where the Marines raised carrots, cabbage, and beans. Groups in the states sent seeds and the Marines gave the seeds and produce from the garden to the Vietnamese to encourage them to diversify their crops and improve their diets. The only barbed wire in the ville protected the garden from water buffalo and the sway-backed pigs.

The footpath led beside a grove of areca trees, across a ravine, to an intersection of three other trails. While Newly and Dig stood watch, Ortega and Mother checked the trails for recent traffic. Finding nothing suspicious, the patrol followed a trail across a stream, along the cemetery, through a bamboo thicket, and along the edge of the ville.

Scarred banana trees and bunkers were all that remained of three hootches that had been destroyed in a firefight between the PFs and Viet Cong. Every hootch had a bunker for the family to hide during the fights and when the Viet Cong dropped mortars on the ville.

"Someone's in this bunker," Ortega said. He stood beside the bunker with a grenade, ready to roll it inside.

"Lai dai," Mother called. Come out. "Didi." Get away. No one came out. "Toss it," he said to Ortega.

"Sounds like someone crying," Ortega said.

"I ain't sticking my head in there," Mother said. "And we ain't leaving until we know."

Ortega thought it over. Fourteen days. "I'm too short," he said. "Lai dai," he called, sticking his finger through the ring on the grenade pin. Still he waited.

"They can't do nothing to me but dig my grave," Dig said. He slowly crawled into the narrow opening holding a cigarette lighter in his hand. When he was half-way in, he wriggled out again. "Girl," he said. "Not from this ville. Having a baby. No weapon." He picked up the machine gun and waited for Ortega to move out.

Ortega took the lighter and looked inside. "She's having trouble," he said.

"She's Viet Cong or she wouldn't be here," Dig said.

"We don't have a corpsman," Mother said.

"It don't mean nothing," Dig said. "What's one more kid in a place like this?"

Ortega looked at Mother. Mother, too, had been one more kid. "Newly, call the squad and tell them exactly where we are and tell them to stand by. Then get first squad's corpsman on the radio and stay close enough I can touch you. Ortega, get over there where you can cover the trail and the ville. Dig, I want the machine gun covering the trail and the paddy."

When Ortega and Dig were in position, Mother turned to Newly. "What did the corpsman say?"

"He said as much as possible leave it up to her. Try to keep her calm. And keep everything clean."

"Clean? There ain't nothing here that's clean. Give me your battle dressing. Get Dig's and Ortega's. I'll wrap the baby in that."

Mother crawled into the bunker. It was damp and close with animal smells. Flicking the lighter he looked at the girl. She looked like a frightened child, her teeth and eyes big, and she made moans and whimpers and little animal sounds.

"There ain't nobody to help but me," he said, reaching out his hand. Her eyes rolled watching his hand, but her head did not move. He laid his hand gently on her forehead and she seemed to shrink under it. Not knowing what else to do he began to sing the first song he could think of. "Hey Jude, don't be afraid, take a sad song and make it better . . ." He could feel her begin to relax. When she closed her eyes, he moved his hand but she caught it and squeezed it in her own.

After a while he crawled outside. "Give me a cigarette," he said. "Tell the corpsman she lost her water. Where's the squad?"

"The squad changed their pos. They're at the pagoda."

"Tell them not to come past the ditch. What are you doing?"

Newly had taken out a lighter and was running it over the blade of his Ka-bar. "Corpsman told me to heat a knife," he said. "Don't touch nothing with it." He handed it to Mother and Mother crawled back inside.

Newly smoked another cigarette, occasionally shrugging when Dig or Ortega looked at him. "He's not breathing," Mother yelled. "Tell the corpsman he's not breathing."

"Mouth to mouth," Newly called. "Doc says give him mouth to mouth."

The next time he emerged, Mother was holding a red, raw, wrinkled thing. "I got me a boy," he said.

"It's eyes ain't even open," Newly said.

"You can't take it with you," Ortega said, appearing beside them. "If you leave it here it ain't got a prayer."

"I thought you was keeping watch," Mother said.

"If there was anybody out there they would have already hit us," Ortega said.

"It ain't even got its eyes open," Newly said.

"If I was born in this country I wouldn't never open my eyes," Ortega said.

"This ain't no real country," Dig said. "Ain't nothing here but hunger and hatred."

"He's alive, ain't he?" Mother said.

"It don't mean nothing. We might as well dig his grave right now," Dig said.

"I breathed life in this kid. Don't tell me it don't mean nothing."

"He may be breathing but he's dead. He ain't never gonna know anything but death and hunger."

"He can choose," Mother said. "As long as he's got breath he can choose. If you want to be dead, you can be dead. He's alive."

"It ain't real," Dig said. "Ain't nothing real in this country except dying."

"You ain't walking dead, you're alive and crawling," Mother said. "You're afraid to live because you're afraid to die. Well, this kid's alive. They can kill him but they can't say he didn't live."

"It's the lieutenant," Newly said, holding up the radio headset. "He's sending the jeep with toys for the kids. He wants us to teach them to play touch football."

"It ain't real," Dig said.

"Maybe it ain't real, but it matters," Mother said. "And don't never tell me again it don't matter. I breathed life in this kid, and that matters. Now give him back to his mama," he said, placing the wet, wriggling thing in Dig's hands.

Dig held the baby before him, as cautiously as if it were a boobytrap. The baby wrinkled its face and began to make little sucking sounds. "This ain't no good place to be born,"

Dig said. "This ain't no good time. There ain't a whole lot out there but grief. And mama." Slowly he sank to his knees before the bunker.

SEASONAL RAIN

It was early summer and the fields were white with harvest. Chris saw the waves of shining wheat, the dark heads turned earthward. He refused to think of it. He had seen the harvest; he had escaped the reaping. He refused to think of that, too. It was no place he wanted to be.

He gave his mind to the heat waves that shimmered on the highway and the pools of water that existed only in his mind. "Don't mean nothing." The words came to him unbidden and he quickly dismissed them. Turning his eyes from the mirage, he considered his plight that left him no faith, no place. For help he could turn to the government or the church. The government would ask questions about his past, the church would ask questions about his future. He had no past that he would discuss and no future that he could see. Behind him was heat, rain, ruin. The future offered the same. He held the only safe ground.

He stood up when the pickup stopped. The driver rolled down the window and the nimbus of cold air offered as little comfort as the pools of water that danced on the highway. "I ain't giving you no ride but I can use you if you can drive a combine."

"I can drive," Chris said, vaguely remembering what a

combine was. He waited under inspection.

"You a hippie? I don't want no hippie."

Chris considered the question. "I ain't nothing," he said, getting into the air-conditioned cab. He shuddered as the cold steel air penetrated his damp shirt.

They drove along the smoothly dipping pavement, past the broad waving fields of grain. "Otto Bachman," the driver said, raising and stiffening his lower lip. He was a short thick man with sloping shoulders and a round head topped by a red cap. He rolled down his window and loosed a brown stream before speaking again. "You don't have no bag." It was not a question so Chris did not answer. "You ever worked before?"

Chris didn't know what to say. He had done a job and he had been paid. His body remembered the days that began and ended in darkness and the darkness that didn't end, but was it work if it came to nothing?

"You're not from around here are you?" Otto asked.

"No."

Otto's head bobbed and his eyes slanted under colorless lashes and brows. "This is a wonderful country when it rains," he said. "I hope to God it don't rain now."

They turned off the highway and onto a blacktop and then onto a sandy lane through the wheat to a weathered frame house; square, squat, and wary under a lifetime metal roof. Three shade trees wilted in the yard, the only trees in sight. Behind the house was a new barn, two metal buildings, and an accumulation of shiny farm equipment. Behind the barn was a scrap heap of obsolete equipment—tractors without motors, mowers without blades, plows without shares.

"You can wash up back there," Otto said, waving vaguely at the house, "and there's a cot on the screened-in porch. It's too hot to cook but I'll fix up some sandwiches while you wash."

Chris walked into the house, down a dark hallway that divided the house in two, and into a small utilitarian bathroom that someone had made hurried but effective efforts to clean. After he had washed, Chris started back down the hall, noticing the bedrooms. In two of them the mattresses were covered with plastic. In the third, the bed was made but without a spread. On the dresser stood a large framed photograph of Otto, a woman, and a boy and girl.

The woman seemed taller and much younger than Otto, with a long, pretty face set for cheerful domesticity. The tall, thin-armed boy pouted beneath his cap and his mother's arm, and the short, round-faced, unhappy girl tried to slide from under her father's arm and out of the picture.

"Out here," Otto called from the screened-in porch. They ate without speaking, washing down bologna sandwiches with iced tea. When he finished, Otto rocked back from the table, pushed a package of cigarettes at Chris, took a pinch of snuff for himself and turned on the radio to listen to the weather report.

Chris finished a third sandwich, eating more slowly now. When he finished, he sat back and lighted a cigarette. How long had it been since the taste of food, the bite of tobacco had been as routine as fear?

Otto snapped off the radio with a snort at the forecast. "I don't want no smoking in the field. Right now that wheat is about to explode. Lightning, the sun shining on broken glass, hot exhaust will set it afire. We lost a combine and two hundred acres of wheat because some damn fool threw a cigarette out of his car. My son was trying to get the combine out of the field. Damn kid." He reset his cap on his head.

Chris looked at the broken-down equipment that stood guard against the night. "I drug it off," Otto said. "I couldn't look at it without getting mad at some fool that would throw out a cigarette with the country as dry as it was. And a damn fool kid getting himself killed trying to save something that didn't have to be saved." He stared at the abandoned equipment and raised his lower lip to dam back the tobacco juice. "I ought to haul it all off, but that don't hurt me to look at. That's something that don't have nothing more to give. Gives me a good feeling remembering it."

Otto spat out the tobacco he had been working on and reset his cap. "Turn out the lights when you turn in."

Chris stretched out on the cot in his clothes. Through the screen he could see the stars, the red winking light of an airplane, fireflies glittering in the night. He turned away. Too many nights had he been awakened by stars bursting in his eyes.

He was awakened in the darkness by an impatient Otto. "Get up, we're already late." They ate bacon and eggs in silence. "You got a hat? You got to have something on your head." He threw Chris a gimme cap.

It was barely light when they reached the combine. Otto greased, oiled, watered, gassed, and checked the machine by hand, instructing Chris. "Feel this, see that, grease those, be sure them are clear." When they finished, Otto tested the wheat, snapping off a few heads and rolling out the grain between his hands. Too tough.

Otto climbed on the machine. "Ever seen one of these things before? That's the reel, knocks the wheat into the blades. If you get the blade too low you pick up trash, too high you miss the grain. The auger feeds the wheat into the beaters, and the beaters shove it into the flails and separate the grain from the straw. The straw walkers dump the straw and chaff out the back. The grain goes up to the hopper. When it's full, I'll pull the truck up to get it. Just keep cutting, I'll pull in real tight."

Otto tested the wheat again. Deciding it was ready, he waved Chris into the seat, gave him instructions on starting the machine and rode with him, shouting into his ear. "Raise the blade. Cut the corner square. Cut around the Johnson grass, I don't want none of that in my seed. Don't leave any wheat. I want a clean field." Chris was relieved when the hopper filled and Otto had to get the deuce-and-a-half.

The sun wore away the day. The heat lay against the land, holding it captive. Only the combine moved, reeling the grain into its open jaws and leaving a row of beaten straw in its wake in an endless cycle around the field.

They did not stop for lunch. Otto climbed onto the combine, handed Chris a bologna sandwich, and dropped off again. Chris followed the path before him with no hope of escape. The sun bleached the earth and burned blood-red behind his eyelids. The thin air stung his nostrils and distended his lungs without giving life. The exhaust from the combine hung in the air, burning his face. Otto came with the truck, loaded, and disappeared. Chris watched the sun slide down the sky, waiting for relief.

The heat did not abate but the sun seemed distant and tired. Christ watched it grow fat and heavy, flattening itself on the horizon. Otto jumped onto the combine and flipped on the lights. "Keep going until it gets too tough to cut," he said.

Chris' muscles ached, his knees trembled from being bent so long, the dust and chaff irritated his skin. The wheat passed from darkness into light then slipped away out of the corners of his eyes. He was startled when Otto jumped on the machine and slapped him on the back. "Kill it," he shouted. Chris shut off the engine and the sudden silence struck like light, stunning his senses.

He dropped stiffly to the ground and stumbled to the pickup through the stubble and straw the combine had left. It wasn't until later that he noticed the sounds of the insects, the wind, distant traffic, other combines working in other fields.

"I took a load to town," Otto said. "Clean sample. No Johnson grass. I'm going to hold some of this back for next year." He reset his cap and spat out the window. "I got you some clothes so you can take a bath. Don't take long because I want to go to town and eat something. We're already late."

Chris showered, washed his hair, pulled on the new

Levis and T-shirt. "Bring your dirty clothes with you," Otto said. "We'll stop at the washateria."

Town was two blocks of service station, cafe, mechanic shop, general store, farm implement store, surrounded by four blocks of frame houses and two churches. Standing over the town like watch towers were the huge grain elevators.

They put Chris's clothes in the washing machine and walked across the street to the Busy Bee Cafe that had four tables and a counter that ran the length of the building. Otto chose a stool at the table.

"Hello, Otto," said the young, red-haired, red-faced, radiantly ugly girl behind the counter. "What chall gonna have?"

"Two burgers, two shakes, and two fries," Otto said. The girl nodded. She was tall for her age, thin and straight as a stalk. Her thin, bony face promised strength in maturity but lacked the dimpled bounty of youth.

Chris realized that Otto and the girl were looking at him. "What chu want?" the girl asked.

While they waited on the orders, Otto teased the girl about school, boys, and red hair. Her face became so red that her freckles looked white, but she did not lose her laugh. She brought their orders and moved to the other end of the counter to provide them seclusion while they ate. "Same age as my daughter," Otto said. "Too ugly to run away."

When he finished, Otto turned around on his stool. "Hell, bring that with you, them clothes is done by now."

Chris picked up his burger and fries and followed Otto

back across the highway. "No need paying for a dryer, just hold them out the window," Otto said, starting the pickup as Chris ran to retrieve his wet clothes.

The days began and ended with the weather report, and were filled with the combine reeling in the waiting wheat. They didn't go back to town and Otto cooked as impatiently as he ate. Afterwards they sat on the porch for a smoke or dip of snuff while Otto consulted the skies, the stars, the almanac, the signs given by animals, rainbows, and insects, and spat his contempt at the weatherman who predicted clear skies. "Any man that can't recognize signs is a damn fool." He spat and reset his cap.

"Now you mind the rain. There ain't nothing a farmer prays for more than rain, and an untimely rain will ruin you quicker than anything. You can always try to outlast a drought. And yet, even when it ruins you, a rain does some good."

Chris remembered a pale wafer floating in cotton wool clouds; the first time he had seen the sun in three weeks. He remembered carrying the children through automatic fire and chest high water. He remembered his clothing rotting, his feet crumbling at the touch. Chris minded the rain.

One morning Otto jumped on the combine and pointed. There was smoke on the horizon, boiling into the sky like an outraged village. "You mind that smoke. If the wind shifts, get this combine out of the field."

Smoke on the horizon, dust devils along unseen farm roads, showers in the distance brought a sense of urgency, but the pace remained the same. By afternoon the cool damp air had made the wheat tough and hard to thrash, and suddenly, without a sound, the rain began. Chris turned the combine towards the house so that it would not be bogged in the field, steering around the standing wheat. By the time he got to the house the rain had slackened and the sun shone through breaks in the clouds. He sat on the porch with Otto watching the thin sheets of rain that glistened in the sunlight.

"I wish if it was going to rain it would rain," Otto said. "A little pissant rain like that don't do nothing but idle you." Otto took a pinch of snuff, tugged at his cap, and watched the rain slant down through the sunlight. "You ever had to sit and watch something you couldn't stand to watch and couldn't do nothing but look?"

"Yes."

Otto looked at him and spat. "That girl of mine was always worrying about the future and it was still the present. She couldn't eat breakfast for worrying about supper. Always going on about how everything was being ruined, like when she was born it was perfect. Just took off. I could see it coming and I couldn't do a damn fool thing about it."

He spat and reset his cap. "Her mama just wasted away. It was a drought. I'd go outside and dead, everything was dead. It looked like the whole world was going to die and blow away. You ever seen it where it looked like the whole world had took sick?"

"Yes."

"I'd come back in the house and she'd say, 'Have you heard from Bobbie Louise?' That's the only thing she ever said. Just lay there looking out the window. Worst drought I ever seen. And now there's rain and it ain't doing nothing but keeping us out of the field." Otto spat. "Let's go to town."

A small carnival had set up in the weeds at the edge of town. Although it was not yet dark, the lights of the whirligig were flashing cheer and the music and shouts of the sideshows drummed excitement. The cafe was filled with combine crews that followed the harvest from the plains of Texas to the plains of Canada. Temporarily idled, paid up and pent up, they lounged the streets like restive and homesick soldiers.

Otto and Chris got hamburgers and malts and sat on the tailgate of the pickup, eating and watching the families coming to town. "I thought I wanted to get married again," Otto said. "She said she didn't want to move out to my place because there wasn't nothing to see. Hell, there ain't nothing out there but scenery. Said there wasn't nothing to do. Hell, you never get ahead of doing. Called me up and said I should see what they done to her hair. So I got dressed and drove over there and she locked her door and went to bed so I couldn't see it. You ever been asked to do something they wouldn't let you do?"

Chris nodded.

They watched the girls, pink and quick as the cotton candy they mouthed. They watched the harvesters drifting to the carnival, following the girls. "Damn fool harvest hands will spend a week's wages to get jubilated by some damn fool girl making them giddy and some damn fool ride making them sick. Go on, I can see you're a mind to." Otto counted out some money. "That's for your first day's work. If you want the rest come and get it. I'm too old to enjoy being foolish and not old enough to enjoy watching."

Chris walked through the dusty weeds beneath the flashing lights. Gunfire crackled, shots pinged off targets, men laughed, girls squealed, figures struggled at the edge of the light, children ran, their shirts flapping like flames beneath the blazing lights.

Chris saw the red-haired, ugly girl standing close to, almost behind a dimpled girl with new-found breasts and eyelashes. Giggling and biting her lips, the dimpled girl succeeded in attracting the attention of a couple of harvesters who swaggered their out-of-townness and said stupid, magical words. Laughing, they led the squealing girl away without a backward look at her less attractive friend. The red-haired girl tried to shrink into the crowd.

"Hi," Chris said. She looked at him with fright, and looked away. "Want to ride the Ferris wheel?" She didn't answer but she let him take her arm and lead her to the Ferris wheel. They rode the tilt-a-whirl and the rocket, went through the fun house. He won her a stuffed pig at the rifle range and bought her cotton candy.

They walked to the edge of the light and leaned against a pickup truck. The lights of the Ferris wheel lingered in her eyes. "You're going to be a beautiful woman," he said.

"Thank you, it's what mama says. It's nice to think I'll be pretty someday but maybe it won't matter then, and it matters now. You ever had people look at you like you reminded them of something they wanted to forget?"

"Yes."

"Mama says don't dwell on April. I'm not going to dwell on being pretty some day and I'm not going to dwell on being ugly now. I'm going to go home and remember this as the nicest night of my life." Awkwardly she kissed him on the cheek and walked away hugging the stuffed pig.

"See anything ripe for cutting?" Otto asked when Chris got back to the pickup.

"No."

Although they were up early the next morning they had to wait several hours before the wheat was dry enough to thrash. Otto fretted over the thunderstorms that bloomed on the horizon. "There's hail in that cloud," Otto said. "We got to get the wheat out."

Chris started the machine and moved the reel into the wheat that nodded and fell before the flashing blades. A brown wall of dust rose in the north, obscuring the horizon, rising into the dark and threatening clouds. The wind sent his cap tumbling across the field, stung tears from his eyes, and snapped his shirt against his back, but he did not stop.

Like the rattle of gunfire, hail stones rang against the metal combine, shattering and bouncing away. He stopped the combine and crawled under it as the hail cut down the ripe wheat. Otto drove the pickup beside the combine, opened the door, and Chris jumped in. They listened to the hail bang against the pickup, watched it dent the hood, beat down the wheat, and cover the ground.

When the hail stopped Otto rolled down his window and looked out at the field white with ruin. "Damn that was good wheat."

"Wasted."

Otto spat out the window. "I always wanted to make things grow," he said. "Damn, it hurts me to see it like this, but that don't wipe out all the times I saw it standing tall and waving in the wind."

"You can't harvest that."

"I'd like to plow this under right now," Otto said. "But it's too tough. I'd like to put some seed in the ground but it's too late to make a crop. Right now I'm a mind to go fishing. Stay until it's time to plow. I know a place if you're a mind."

"I'm a mind," Chris said. He got out of the pickup and walked to the combine, the hail crunching under his feet. He started the engine, raised the blade, and cut straight across the field to the house, having no mind for the waste behind him.

THE DOG THAT KNEW BETTER

Otis got the dog because he didn't want to have to buy his daughter a birthday present. Otis Hopkins, Wanderer Springs' only banker, was not a stingy man, but every store in town was in debt to him, and if he bought anything from them he would be buying goods they had bought with his money. Otis was a fiscal conservative.

The people who had dogs also owed Otis money, but in Wanderer Springs no one bought or sold dogs. In Wanderer Springs dogs were like oleanders. Anybody who had one gave cuttings to anybody who wanted one. There were enough oleanders for everybody.

Otis selected the puppy the way he selected everything from mortgages to slices of pie; he took the biggest one in the litter. The puppy was not quite yellow, not quite brown. Not big but heavy-bodied with short legs and enormous snowshoe paws. He was not longhaired except for whiskers that bristled around his muzzle.

Otis named the dog "Dudley" after the man who gave him the dog, a free haircut, shave, shoe shine, and assurances he would not fall in debt again. Otis was solicitous.

Otis also cared about his only daughter, Wanda. Wanda had no mother, no brothers, no sisters. She was too young to go to school. Otis would not let her play with other children because their parents owed him money, and Otis did not want to dispossess the parents of his daughter's friends. Otis was sentimental.

Like her father, Wanda was fat, but unlike her father, Wanda was not cheerful. Wanda was sullen. Wanda had nothing to do but play with the dolls she could not take outside, eat bread, butter, and jam, stamp her foot at the woman who kept house, and stick out her tongue at Otis when he came home. Wanda was precocious.

Wanda needed someone to love. Wanda needed someone to frolic with. Wanda was delighted to see Dudley. However, Dudley was not a lovable dog. Dudley did not jump up and down excited to see her. He did not put his head under her arm. He was not attentive to her secrets. He licked her face and hands only when she was eating bread, butter, and jam.

Dudley was not frolicsome. Dudley did not play chase, follow the leader, or hide and go seek. Dudley understood his name only when he was called to eat. Then he roused himself rather than rose, and padded off in a curious sideways manner with his bristly, oversized head cocked. Dudley was a laying-around, doll-eating, shoe-chewing kind of dog.

"You know better than that," Otis yelled at the dog as he beat Dudley with one of the canvas sacks the bank kept money in. Such tactics did not seem to work.

Otis drove Dudley into the country, opened the door, pushed the dog out, and drove away. He hoped if the dog didn't starve someone would take him in.

Nearby was the farmhouse of Emil Drieschner. Emil was a good farmer. Emil's sons had left home to find easier work. Emil's daughters had left home to find more interesting lives. Emil's wife had taken to her bed. Emil was a hard worker.

Dudley found his way to Emil's farmhouse. Emil was delighted to see the dog. Emil tried to train Dudley to guard the chickens and bring in the cows at milking time. Dudley was not a working dog. Dudley was an egg-sucking, chicken-killing, cow-chasing kind of dog. "You know better than that," Emil yelled. He stuffed hot peppers in the eggs and made Dudley eat them. He tied a dead chicken around Dudley's neck and let it rot. Such tactics did not seem to work.

Emil drove Dudley to town and dumped him, hoping that if he didn't get run over someone would take him in. Dudley found his way back to Wanda. Otis drove him to the country and dropped him. Dudley found his way back to Emil. Dudley was a slow learner.

One day Wanda escaped the fence that was supposed to keep kidnappers from stealing her, and wandered down to the creek, a place she had been told never to go. Wanda threw rocks at birds, stamped on frogs, and chased insects into the water. So rapt was Wanda in chasing the insects that she fell into the creek. Wanda was absorbed.

Wanda's screams brought other children to the creek but they could not swim. Wanda would have drowned had not Dudley, on one of his tours from the farm to the city, heard Wanda, jumped into the creek, caught her dress in his strong but underslung jaw, and pulled her to safety.

The children jumped up and down, laughing and clapping their hands. Wanda stamped her foot, stuck out her tongue, and ran crying to the house, forgetting Dudley. Wanda was vain.

Hearing her cries, Otis ran to meet her, picked her up, and holding her at arm's length, carried her to a bath, forgetting Dudley. Otis was neat.

Dudley would have been forgotten had not the children told the mayor of the rescue. The mayor thought of having the dog displayed at the fire station, where the city council met. The mayor thought of having the city buy a gold medal for the mayor to present to the dog. The mayor thought of having the paper take pictures of him presenting the medal to the dog. The mayor was thoughtful.

Dudley was displayed at the fire station and people came to view him. The mayor proclaimed the dog a hero and people came to hear him. Otis had to buy a brass-studded collar for Dudley so the mayor could attach the gold medal to it. Wanda had to kiss Dudley so the newspaper could take her picture. Otis and Wanda were winsome.

Dudley was a hero and Otis and Wanda had to take the dog home with them. But Dudley was not content. Dudley was a big, maladjusted dog that could not adapt to the rigors of civilization. Dudley did not frolic with Wanda. Dudley did not listen to Wanda's complaints. Dudley went to the creek and rescued a drowned chicken. Dudley was a one-trick dog.

Otis returned the chicken to the creek and washed his hands before beating Dudley with a money bag. "You know better than that," he yelled. The tactic worked no better than before.

In the dead of night, Otis delivered Dudley to the country. He told everyone he had donated the dog to the American Red Cross for life-saving work. Otis was smart.

Dudley went back to Emil's, taking with him a sodden picnic basket, leaving a trail of sodden picnic. Emil knew the dog was a hero. Emil knew that Otis Hopkins had lied about the dog. Emil knew that some day he might need to borrow money from Otis. Emil was smart. Instead of returning the dog to town, Emil left Dudley at the river, near the old bridge, hoping if he didn't drown he would be happy.

Nearby was the dugout of the Hight boys. The Hight boys had first names like everybody else but the two of them were always together so no one ever bothered to distinguish between them. They were old but everybody called them the Hight "boys" because no one took them seriously. They hunted and fished for food. They made stink-bait from the animals run over on the highway that crossed the bridge, and sold it to fishermen for the few coins they needed. The Hights were not civilized.

Dudley found his way to the Hight boys' dugout. Dudley rescued the back seat of an automobile from the river and dragged it to the dugout and lay down on it. The Hights saw Dudley the way they saw the river. They did not feed Dudley. They did not train him to hunt. They did not take him with them when they fished under the bridge. They lived in proximity to Dudley. The Hights were not acquisitive.

Dudley rescued a tow sack from the river, an old shirt, a good shoe. What Dudley did not use the Hights took. What the Hights did not use, they took downstream and threw in the river when Dudley was asleep. Dudley was a collector.

One day it rained up in the Panhandle. Two days later the river was flooding below the Hight dugout, heavy with debris. Dudley stayed at the river day and night working until he was exhausted. Dudley recognized destiny.

It was near dusk on the second day when Dudley saw a soggy mattress skimming along the river, mostly under water on one side. The river was running fast but Dudley swam after the mattress and caught it in his undershot muzzle. Only his bristly head was above water as he tugged at the mattress, his feet paddling furiously in that curious sideways motion, his eyes rolled back so they were mostly white. Dudley was ambitious.

The Hights saw the dog and the mattress and followed. They watched the struggle the way they watched the river. They stopped short of the old bridge because a crowd had gathered to watch the bridge wash away. The Hights shrugged their shoulders, turned their backs on the crowd and walked away. The Hights were not sociable.

Otis Hopkins was at the bridge, and Wanda, and Emil Drieschner, and the mayor who had given Dudley a medal. They saw Dudley and the mattress and called him to give up the mattress and come to them. Dudley seemed not to hear.

Young boys saw the dog and mattress and threw rocks at the dog to knock him loose from his prize. Because, even though he was not their dog, he was still a dog. They were young.

Dudley would not let go although it was obvious he could not get the mattress to the bank. Dudley was being dragged by the mattress, dragged down as the mattress got heavier. Only his eyes and the bristles around his nose were above water, kept there by the furious sideways paddle of his snowshoe paws. Dudley aspired.

The mattress folded up and disappeared under the water, pulling the undershot muzzle and wide, white eyes with it. Still Dudley did not let go. Maybe it was because he had gone too far to covet safety. Maybe it was because, even though the mattress was lost, it was still the biggest thing he had ever gotten his teeth into. Dudley was an artist.

Otis Hopkins thought about the brass studded collar. Wanda thought about the gold medal. The mayor thought about the crowd that had come to the fire station to see him give the dog a medal. Emil thought about working so hard for so little. The others at the bridge thought about dying for something as useless as a shapeless mattress. No one believed Dudley was a hero. They believed he knew better.